ZOE MINISTRIES INTERNATIONAL

HOW TO FOLLOW GOD'S VOICE
IN INTERCESSION

STUDY GUIDE

WWW.ZOEMINISTRIES.ORG

Copyright © 1998, 2016
All rights reserved.

This Study Guide or parts thereof may not be reproduced, stored or transmitted in any form by any means without prior written permission of ZOE Ministries International, except as provided by United States of America copyright law.

ZOE Ministries International
P.O. Box 2207
Arvada, CO 80001-2207 USA
permissions@zoemin.org

Rev. 03/23

ACKNOWLEDGEMENTS

ZOE Ministries International is dedicated to training, equipping and sending believers into the world to minister by the leading of the Holy Spirit. This ministry helps build the body of Christ and encourages God's people to use their gifts and talents for His glory. It is for this purpose that this publication has been compiled by the leading of the Holy Spirit and the input of many people. ZOE Ministries wishes to thank them for their support, time, and talents in contributing to this study guide. We give our Lord all the praise and glory for this work!

CONTENTS

Course Outline 7

Lesson 1   Introduction 21

Lesson 2   The Need for Intercession 33

Lesson 3   Jesus, Our Intercessor 49

Lesson 4   The Holy Spirit and Intercession 63

Lesson 5   Perseverance and Holiness 73

Lesson 6   Intercession for the Family 83

Lesson 7   Praying for People Groups 91

Lesson 8   My God Will Hear Me 101

Lesson 9   Travailing and Prevailing Intercession 111

Lesson 10   Intercession of Paul 125

Lesson 11   God Is Searching for Intercessors 129

Lesson 12   Preparing for the Coming Revival 135

ZOE Course Descriptions 141

Magazine List 144

HOW TO FOLLOW GOD'S VOICE—IN INTERCESSION

COURSE OUTLINE

Lesson 1   **INTRODUCTION**
  Class Articles:
  - *Why Pray?*, B.J. Willhite
  - *Make Me An Intercessor*, P. Tan
  - *Shaping History And Ourselves*, J. Dawson

Lesson 2   **THE NEED FOR INTERCESSION**
  Scripture: **Isaiah 62:6–7; Luke 11:1–13**
  Murray: Introduction; Chapters 1 and 3
  Assigned Articles:
  - *Passionate Prayer*, M. Caulk
  - *Why Prayer Is My Priority*, T. Barnett
  - *The Language Of Intercession*, C. Jacobs

Lesson 3   **JESUS, OUR INTERCESSOR**
  Scripture: **Hebrews 4:12 through 5:14; John 17:9–24; John 15:7**
  Murray: Chapters 5 and 11
  Assigned Articles:
  - *Focus On Jesus*, B. Shull
  - *The Three Purposes For Intercessory Prayer*, R. Mahoney
  - *Prayer That Is Pleasing To The Lord*, D. Wilkerson

Lesson 4   **THE HOLY SPIRIT AND INTERCESSION**
  Scripture: **Romans 8:1–27**
  Murray: Chapters 2 and 10
  Assigned Articles:
  - *The Listening Side Of Prayer*, S. Padrick
  - *Flaky Intercession*, C. Jacobs

Lesson 5   **PERSEVERANCE AND HOLINESS**
  Scripture: **Joshua 7; Luke 18:1–8; Revelation 5:8; 8:3–5**
  Murray: Chapters 4 and 6
  Assigned Articles:
  - *Who Are You?*, B. Shull
  - *Consecration: A Partnership With The Lord*, K. Henry
  - *Finding God In Your Wilderness*, A. Smith

Lesson 6   **INTERCESSION FOR THE FAMILY**
  Scripture: **Esther; Galatians 4:19**
  Murray: Chapter 7
  Assigned Articles:
  - *Intercession*, K. Henry
  - *Courage In The Inner Court*, D. Prince
  Study Help: "Scriptures For Prayer For The Family" ZOE Ministries

Lesson 7   **PRAYING FOR PEOPLE GROUPS**
  Scripture: **Genesis 18:16 through 19:29**
  Murray: Chapter 8
  Assigned Articles:
  - *How To Pray For The Lost*, D. Sheets
  - *Pray Until Something Happens*, D. Stringer

HOW TO FOLLOW GOD'S VOICE—IN INTERCESSION

Lesson 8   **MY GOD WILL HEAR ME**
                 Scripture: **1 Kings 18:1–40**
                 Murray: Chapter 12
                 Assigned Articles: *Hear God's Voice*, L. LeSourd
                                       Arouse Thyself To Prayer, M. Bickle
                                       The Power Of Early Prayer, B. Bosworth

Lesson 9   **TRAVAILING AND PREVAILING INTERCESSION**
                 Scripture: **Jeremiah 9; 1 Kings 18:41–46; James 5:13–20**
                 Murray: Chapter 9
                 Assigned Articles: *All Manner Of Prayer*, B. Shull
                                       Travailing In Prayer, C. Jacobs
                                       Why Is It So Hard For Christians To Pray?, D. Wilkerson

Lesson 10   **INTERCESSION OF PAUL**
                 Scripture: **Colossians 1:3, 9–12; Ephesians 1:15–23; 3:14–21**
                 Murray: Chapter 13
                 Assigned Articles: *I Interceded In The Spirit During My 'Prayer Dreams'*, P. Harthern

Lesson 11   **GOD IS SEARCHING FOR INTERCESSORS**
                 Scripture: **Nehemiah 1; 2 Corinthians 4**
                 Murray Chapter 14
                 Assigned Articles: *This Prayer Group Is Driving Me Crazy*, E. Smith

Lesson 12   **PREPARING FOR THE COMING REVIVAL**
                 Scripture: **Joel 2**
                 Murray: Chapter 15
                 Assigned Articles: *Prayer—Our High Privilege*, F. Huegel
                                       Loving Enough To Intercede, B. Eslin

Study Materials:
1. Bible, any version
2. The Ministry of Intercessory Prayer, Andrew Murray, Bethany House Publishers, Minneapolis, Minnesota, 1981.
3. Various Articles in the Study Guide
   a. Class Article - to be read in class
   b. Assigned Article - to be read in preparation for class
   c. Study Help—for the participant's use in studying at home

FOREWORD

Dear Participant,

Welcome to this ZOE Intercession course!

So many times in the past we have heard, "I really can't get into praying for others, my country, the nations," OR "Many times I want to fall asleep in my own prayer time or even in prayer meetings," OR "My mind wanders off to my 'to do list.'" Maybe you too have had this experience?

However, we believe that the Lord is increasingly placing a burden on the hearts of men and women to pray as the days continue to grow darker. We realize our hearts are being touched by the Holy Spirit to fall to our knees and pray for the darkness that, in an unprecedented way, is coming against our children and family. Persecution is increasing, and the desire for intercession is being set aflame by the Spirit of God.

We believe this course will not only challenge you to intercede for all your needs, but will "set a fire in your bones," Jeremiah 20:9. A passion will enter your heart to go into intercession in areas that you have never thought of before.

This course will prove to be such a sweet time together with other praying believers, as you pray in agreement about the main principle for each lesson.

We have had testimonies from individuals who have taken this course, expressing their desire to stay together and continue to touch the heart of God with prayers that are led by the Holy Spirit.

It is our prayer that through this course, you too will be touched, encouraged and given a hunger for more of the Lord's heart in all areas of your lives.

May God bless you greatly!

For His Glory,

Dick and Ginny Chanda
Founding Directors

A NOTE TO COURSE PARTICIPANTS

What ZOE Is!

1. A ministry that provides training for disciple-making.
2. Participatory classes where all are encouraged to share and contribute.
3. A situation where the leader (facilitator) decreases and the participants increase.
4. A drawing out of ministry gifts and preparation for the Lord's calling on individual lives.
5. A time when one can grow in the understanding and appreciation of others' gifts.
6. A safe environment in which an individual can feel comfortable to practice operating in his or her gifts.
7. A time of understanding the heart of the Father and applying that to one's life.

What ZOE Is Not!

1. A traditional Bible study.
2. A course where the leader speaks and the people take notes.
3. A place where people can air their opinions or gripes.
4. A place where people can discuss church doctrines.
5. A time when "weird" ministry happens.

A Reminder to Participants:

"A ZOE class is not just a Bible study; our leader is a facilitator and coach, not a teacher."

It is our desire that the Lord Jesus Christ be glorified in all that is said and done in ZOE classes. We wish to foster an understanding of the operation of His Holy Spirit and to yield to His workings.

HOW TO FOLLOW GOD'S VOICE—IN INTERCESSION

MAIN PRINCIPLES

Lesson 1: As intercessors, we act as a mediator and seek the Father's heart on the behalf of others. Allowing faith to rise in our spirits, we can speak forth the prayers the Holy Spirit guides us to pray. Then, because our prayer is in agreement with God's plan, we can sit back and watch the Lord accomplish it.

Lesson 2: We need to realize the importance of intercessory prayer. It can change our life and the world around us.

Lesson 3: Knowing, believing and abiding in the Word of God, imparts to us an intercessory prayer life parallel to Christ's—of asking and receiving all for the glory of God. Successful intercessory prayer is the fruit of a surrendered life of abiding in Christ.

Lesson 4: God is eager to give the Holy Spirit to those who ask. The Holy Spirit prays with us and for us according to God's will. God still seeks those who will specially give themselves to prayer guided by the Holy Spirit.

Lesson 5: We must walk in holiness before the Lord so that our prayers can be effective. Persistence and perseverance have an important role in our prayer life.

Lesson 6: We have the honor and responsibility of praying for our families. As we intercede on behalf of our family, we need to ask God what His hopes and plans are for them, and pray accordingly.

Lesson 7: It is on the heart of God that His people pray for the Holy Spirit to snatch many people groups around the world from the judgment awaiting them. He desires that all would come to a saving faith in His Son Jesus. Though God can do whatever He wishes, He has chosen to use us as His vessels for His glory.

Lesson 8: God wants us to pray the prayer of faith, with a solid vision of Him as our living and awesome God, who is waiting not only to hear, but also to grant our request.

Lesson 9: Effective travailing and prevailing prayer comes from belief in Jesus' words in Mark 11:24: ". . . Whatever you ask for in prayer, believe that you have received it, and it will be yours." Travailing and prevailing intercessors allow God to place His desire in their hearts and then continue praying in faith for God's desire, despite all obstacles, until it is established.

Lesson 10: We can look at Paul's example and gain a pattern of prayer for our own lives. Paul's prayers reveal the depth of relationship he maintained with the Lord. Paul received much from God, and he desired that the people for whom he labored would also receive abundantly.

Lesson 11: Intercession is foundational to action, and action completes intercession. As we seek God's direction and pray, we must follow through in obedience and be willing to carry out God's plans

Lesson 12: The on-going prayer of the Church should be one of repentance and desire for a fresh awakening to life in Christ. The Lord said that in the latter days He would pour out His Spirit on all flesh. Whether this fulfillment of prophecy is around the corner or some time away, let us pray that the Lord will move on our land in this way.

HOW TO FOLLOW GOD'S VOICE—IN INTERCESSION

PARTICIPANT'S RESPONSIBILITIES

I. Class Preparation

    A. **Read the assigned scriptures and come prepared to share in class.**

        1. Ask the Holy Spirit, **"Open my eyes that I may see wonderful things in Your law." Psalm 119:18** You may be very familiar with the assigned Scriptures, but the Lord is very faithful and can give you "fresh manna."

        2. Look at the Main Principle for the lesson and apply the Scriptures. Ask yourself the following questions:
            a. How does this Scripture apply to the lesson?
            b. How does this Scripture apply to my life?
            c. What do I need to do to apply this Scripture to my life and to the lives of others for God's glory?

    B. **Read the assigned chapters or pages in the book and come prepared to share in the class.**
    Note in your book any thoughts related to the Main Principle for the lesson.

    C. **Read the assigned articles and come prepared to share in the class.**
    Note any thoughts related to the Main Principle for the lesson.

    D. **Maintain a journal—a valuable tool in God's hands.**
    As you learn to hear God's voice and keep a record of His speaking, you will become more aware of what He is saying to you and how He wants to work through you. See the article "Journaling—A Good Way to Hear God's Voice."

    E. **Spend time in prayer.**
        1. Prayer is valuable preparation for these classes. The more time you spend with the Lord, the more you will come to know Him.
        2. Spend time with God <u>daily</u>! Avoid crash studying. God shows no partiality—what He has done for others, He will do for you! Growth will come as you respond to God's Holy Spirit at work in your life.

II. Class Participation

    A. Training is active! You will be encouraged to **take part in the class discussions and the prayer and ministry time.**

    B. You will have the opportunity to **lead the discussion** of the assigned reading as you feel comfortable. No one will be forced to lead—only encouraged! Discussion Leader assignments are made two weeks in advance so that you have ample time to prepare. There is a helpful handout on leading class discussions in your Study Guide.

JOURNALING – A GOOD WAY TO HEAR GOD'S VOICE

What Goes Into a Journal?

1. Your thoughts—impressions, insights, hopes, fears, goals, struggles.
2. Your feelings—both positive and negative.
3. Your prayers and answers to prayer.
4. Excerpts from Scripture and other reading that God seems to be highlighting for you.

How to Journal

1. You may choose to use a spiral binder or a hardback blank book, or anything that you can take with you easily on trips.
2. Journal every day, if possible, during the time that you read Scripture and pray. Record in it insights that the Lord gave you that day or the day before.
3. You may want to keep a separate section in your journal for prayers or excerpts from your reading.
4. Write directly to God as if you were talking to Him or writing Him a letter.

The Benefits of Keeping a Journal are Many

1. Journaling fosters a readiness to hear from God. Personal communion with God takes place as you write out your thoughts and feelings, and record the insights and impressions He gives you.
2. As you read God's Word and record your insights about Scripture, God is faithful to provide the admonitions, encouragement and guidance that you need.
3. Prayers become specific as you place them in print. In addition, God gets the glory when you review your journal and see your prayers have been answered.
4. Journaling helps clarify your thinking. Fears and struggles are more clearly defined so that they can be dealt with.
5. During times of discouragement, it can help to look back over your journal and see God's faithfulness and your progress in spiritual growth.

HOW TO FOLLOW GOD'S VOICE—IN INTERCESSION

GUIDELINES FOR LEADING A COURSE DISCUSSION

1. Prayer

As you study the assigned material, ask God for insights. Ask Him to show you the main points to be discussed and questions to ask to aid the discussion. Come a few minutes early to the class and pray with the Facilitators before the class begins.

2. Maintain Control of the Discussion

After the class has been turned over to you by the Facilitators, you are to maintain control of the discussion.
   a. Do not allow one or two participants to dominate the discussion time.
   b. Stick to the subject. God may give you many insights, but keep the discussion related to the Main Principle of the lesson.

3. Work Within the Allotted Time

For a 2½ hour course:
   Approximately 30 minutes for the book
   Approximately 50 minutes for the Scripture discussion
   Approximately 15 minutes for the articles
      (Allowing 20 min. for the Facilitators to lead the prayer/ministry)

For a 1½ hour course:
   Approximately 20 minutes for the book
   Approximately 30 minutes for the Scripture discussion
   Approximately 10 minutes for the articles
      (Allowing 10 min. for the Facilitators to lead the prayer/ministry)

ZOE courses focus on what God says through the Bible. Be careful not to spend too much time on the book or articles, which are provided only as supplements to the Scriptures.

4. Encourage Discussion

Course members should be prepared to share insights that the Lord gave them while they read the assigned material. You may need to draw out these insights by asking questions.
   a. Begin with a *launch* question, a broad question that can be answered in a number of different ways by anyone in the group.
   b. Then use *guide* questions, which are short questions that keep the discussion moving in a direction that is related to the Main Principle of that lesson. Life application of the principles found in the assigned reading should be a focus during some part of the discussion.
   c. To close the discussion time, summarize very briefly the main points of the discussion.

May God bless you as you study and pray in preparation for the course. We will be praying for you as you prepare. We love and appreciate you. ~*The Facilitators*

LESSON 1

INTRODUCTION

MAIN PRINCIPLE

As intercessors, we act as a mediator and seek the Father's heart on the behalf of others. Allowing faith to rise in our spirits, we can speak forth the prayers the Holy Spirit guides us to pray. Then, because our prayer is in agreement with God's plan, we can sit back and watch the Lord accomplish it.

DISCLAIMER

The articles that follow have been chosen to give you, the reader, a broader perspective on many of the issues presented in the course. All the ideas in these articles do not necessarily represent the views of *ZOE Ministries International*. However, we pray that as you read and study, you will glean a sense of what is in the author's heart. At all times we need to ask the question, "Does this line up with the Word of God?"

HOW TO FOLLOW GOD'S VOICE - IN INTERCESSION

WHY PRAY?

by B.J. Willhite

WHY WOULD AN OMNIPOTENT, OMNISCIENT GOD NEED US TO PRAY? CAN'T HE DO WHAT HE WANTS WITHOUT US?

Larry Lea has risen as a prominent teacher on prayer in recent years. Thousands of people have read his books and attended his seminars. But where did Larry Lea learn about prayer? Of course, he learned a lot from the Bible and from God. But Lea says that his prayer mentor, the man who pointed him in the right direction and has helped him along the way, is B.J. Willhite.

Willhite has preached at country churches in Texas for years. More recently he has moved to Washington, D.C., and opened the international Prayer Embassy. There prayers intercede for the nation and the world. Also, prayer requests are dispatched around the world via shortwave radio.

Willhite has written a book about prayer. Titled, Why Pray? It is scheduled to be released by Creation House this month. The following is an excerpt from that book.

Does God lack something that we can contribute to Him; does He have some insufficiency that we can supply through our prayer? Several years ago I began to ask myself, "Why pray?" Frankly, I could not find an answer.

I read most of the classics on prayer and found that they said almost the same things; they discussed different kinds of prayer, including the how-to of prayer, but none seemed to go into the why of prayer.

As I began to analyze my own prayers, I saw that most of what I was calling prayer was not prayer at all. As I listened to myself and others pray, I realized one would get the impression that God didn't know very much. Prayer seemed to be an informing session, where I told God about things that perhaps He had overlooked. Sometimes prayer was an instruction session, where I would tell God how He should deal with certain matters. It was as though He would not know just what to do unless He had my suggestions or directions. At other times I heard myself praying as if God were not as concerned about a matter as He should be. It was my duty to somehow stir Him up to where His concern would equal mine. As these patterns became obvious, I began to realize that much of my prayer time was an exercise in futility.

To understand the purpose of prayer you must know how God implements His will in this universe, and to understand that we must go back to the beginning.

"In the beginning God created the heavens and the earth" (Gen. 1:1, NKJV). Paul tells us: "By Him (Jesus) all things were created that are in heaven and that are on earth, visible and invisible, whether thrones or dominions or principalities or powers. All things were created through Him and for Him. And He is before all things, and in Him all things consist" (Col. 1:16,17). Every part of the creation was created in perfect order and balance, sustained and held together by Christ. God did not create the fish before He created the water. First grass was created, then the cattle. God built into His creation an amazing interdependence. Each living thing depends upon other living things, and the whole community of living things has a corporate dependence on the environment.

The universe God created was designed to function under a system of law: natural, physical laws—and spiritual laws. Those who study such matters tell

January 1989, Charisma

us there are multiplied billions of systems like our own Milky Way, each with its billions of stars orbiting around the center of the universe. And every planet revolves around its sun and is held in its place—by law. Our God created it all and He Himself operates within the laws He established. He does not change the length of the days. He does not make a decision about weather. Those things are determined by law. When warm, moisture-laden air meets a cool front, clouds will form and precipitation will fall. Nothing supernatural about it. That is the law. And God Himself does not supersede those laws unless it can be done legally.

Up until the sixth creative day all was well and good. But on the sixth day, God created a potential problem:

"Then God said, 'Let Us make man in Our image, according to Our likeness. And let them have dominion over the fish of the sea, over the birds of the air, and over the cattle, over all the earth and over every creeping thing that creeps on the earth.' So God created man in His own image, in the image of God He created him; male and female He created them. Then God blessed them, and God said to them, "Be fruitful and multiply; fill the earth and subdue it; have dominion over the fish of the sea, over the birds of the air, and over every living thing that moves on the earth"' (Gen. 1:26-28).

When God created man and woman and placed them upon the earth, He gave them dominion over every living thing. Though we do not find anywhere in the Word that man was given "free will," we believe that he was because of the way he was dealt with. Genesis 2:16 shows that Adam was given the right to decide whether or not he would obey God's command. He was not forced to obey or to disobey. The choice was his, though he was told the price of disobedience. Genesis 3:1-6 tells the story of the decision that was made and how Adam and Eve disobeyed God.

Adam's decision did not catch God off guard. He, who knows all, knew what Adam would do. But Adam's sin did present a problem. How could a sovereign God, in a universe governed by natural law, implement His will in a world under the dominion of a rebel to whom he had given a free will?

There's a question with which theologians have struggled for centuries: How can God be truly sovereign and man truly free? Most have adopted the position that if mankind is free, God is not sovereign; holding to the sovereignty of God, they conclude that mankind isn't really free. It is my conviction that both are possible: mankind is free *and* God is sovereign. In fact, I believe it was for this very reason that God established the highest law of the universe—a law that would guarantee His sovereignty and mankind's free will.

The law of gravity is a high law, but not the highest. I got on an airplane in Washington, D.C., the other day and, though that airplane and its cargo weighed hundreds of tons, it rolled down the runway at National Airport, climbed to 35,000 feet and came rushing toward Seattle at 550 miles per hour. As the pilot gently reduced the speed, we landed on the runway safe and sound, not once breaking the law of gravity. The laws of velocity and aerodynamics worked together to *overcome* the pull of gravity.

What does this have to do with prayer?

The law of prayer is the highest law of the universe—it can overcome the other laws by sanctioning God's intervention. When implemented properly the law of prayer permits God to exercise His sovereignty in a world under the dominion of a rebel with a free will, in a universe governed by natural law.

There are those among the rebels who have chosen of their own free will to obey God. They want His will to be done more than their own. So they pray, "Thy kingdom come. Thy will be done in earth as in heaven." As they pray that prayer, they set up the conditions under which God can legally impose His will in a given situation.

Pharaoh did not want to release the people of Israel. It was not his will to do so. It was, however, the will of God. As the people prayed, the Lord sent a deliverer. He intervened in opposition to the will of Pharaoh. As you read through the Scriptures, you see this principle working over and over again.

The book of Joshua records the story of the Israelites possessing the land God had promised Abraham as an eternal inheritance. During one fierce battle with the Amorites, they needed more daylight in order to complete the rout. As Joshua consulted with the Lord about the matter, he evidently was told what to do. Joshua came out of the place of prayer and commanded the sun to stand still. It did—for almost a full day according to Joshua 10:13. Joshua, through prayer, determined the will of God about the matter; he was told what to do; he did it and the battle was won. He made it lawful for God to supersede natural law and do what was necessary to extend the length of a day. It happened because a man knew God's will and did it.

You think you need a longer day? Don't try it. Joshua did not come up with a bright idea and then ask God to make it work. He got his idea from God. When God tells us to do something, it will be successful, not once in a while, but every time. I do not mean to imply

January 1989, Charisma

that there will be no problems. The truth is, there may be many.

Moses was in the will of God when he went to deliver Israel from Egyptian bondage, but it was not an easy task. At times it seemed as though the whole idea was a mistake. Just when it seemed they had finally been released and were on their way to the Promised Land, Pharaoh changed his mind and led his army in pursuit. Behind were the Pharaoh and his army; ahead was the Read Sea. It seemed there was no way out. Something supernatural would have to happen and it did.

Moses was a prayer, always talking to God, and God was always talking with him. The situation was desperate. They needed a miracle, but not once did Moses tell God what He should do. Moses spoke to the people, who were already beginning to complain: "Do not be afraid. Stand still, and see the salvation of the Lord, which He will accomplish for you today. For the Egyptian whom you see today, you shall see again no more forever" (Ex. 14:13). Then the Lord told Moses what to do: "Lift up your rod and stretch out your hand over the sea and divide it" (14:16). That he did, and the water's parted, allowing the whole nation to cross on dry land. Moses' prayer and faith set up the conditions under which God could do what He was going to do. It is not clear whether or not Moses knew exactly what God was going to do, but he knew God would do something. Do you see what I am saying?

The prayer of faith makes it possible for God to do what He wills to do. Prayer does not generally change the mind of God, though there have been times when it has. It more often allows Him to do His will.

Our first building at Church on the Rock was in the very last stages of completion. Announcements of the opening services had gone out and the people were very excited—especially since they were moving in debt-free. Then the city building inspector came to make a final check before issuing the occupancy permit. Everything was exactly right in the building, but he said the ditch carrying our sewer line to the main line was filled with the wrong size of gravel. One Wednesday before the opening Sunday service, he ordered the ditch to be dug out and the gravel replaced. Machinery was immediately brought in and the work began. It could be completed by Sunday—if the weather cooperated.

Saturday came and everything was going well. It seemed the work would be finished by nightfall. But the sky toward the southwest began to darken and streaks of lightning were seen—it was raining on Lake Ray Hubbard, only two miles west, coming down in sheets. And the rain was headed straight toward Rockwall.

When the rain was less than a mile away, the workmen headed for cover; but the foreman, a member of the church said, "Don't stop. It isn't going to rain on this property today."

Well, it did rain west and north of where the work was going on, but not there. Why? "The pastor is praying," the foreman said. Prayer had allowed God to legally impose His will in the matter and move the clouds around.

You may ask, "Can I change the weather if I pray?" Probably not. However, if it is something that will bring glory to God and is a part of His plan, it will be done as we pray. You must understand the "if" factor, which is always there. God cannot answer every prayer we pray. Not because He does not have the ability, but because it is not His will. Nowhere has God promised to answer every prayer we pray. Things would be in a real mess if He did.

Many years ago the Arkansas football team beat Nebraska in the Cotton Bowl. After the game one of my deacons said, "I knew they were going to win."

"How did you know that?" I asked.

"I prayed for them…" he quickly responded."

"But," I said, "don't you think there were people praying for Nebraska to win?"

"Yes," he answered, "but I prayed first."

Of course he was only joking, but it does illustrate a point. If the weather were controlled by people's prayers, we would have serious troubles. Having said that, I wouldn't want you to believe that the weather cannot be changed by God in answer to the prayer of His people. The skeptics may not believe it, but I am sure it has been in the past and will be in the future.

While in Florida I heard the story of a hurricane that had been heading right toward Miami. It was a big one and if it hit, there was certainly going to be much damage and possibly loss of life. As it neared the coast, many Christians gathered and began to pray that the course of the hurricane would be altered. Suddenly it stopped, and just remained in the same place for hours as if gathering momentum for an attack. The people kept praying; it was almost as if a battle was going on. Then eventually it moved, but not toward the coast. It went off the northeast without causing any serious trouble. Did prayer change things?…[missing text].

[In Matthew 9:37 Jesus said, "The harvest is plentiful,] but the laborers are few." I am sure He is saying those same words to His followers today—there

January 1989, Charisma

are more lost sheep than ever. And compared to the magnitude of the harvest, laborers are still scarce.

But Jesus said more. He gave His disciples a strange directive: "Therefore pray that the Lord of the harvest will send laborers into his harvest." Why did He tell us to pray? Surely we can do better than that. If there is a shortage of laborers, why not begin classes of evangelism? Or call the best evangelist we can find? Announce an evangelical crusade. Call in gifted musicians. Spread the word far and wide. Hand out invitations. Knock on every door in the community. We just have to do something about bringing in the harvest. But pray? That is what Jesus said to do. Yes, pray. Pray! We have done about everything except pray, though we do a little of that also: "Lord, now bless our best efforts, we pray, in Jesus' name, Amen."

All of the above things may be all right, but they are not what Jesus instructed us to do. Perhaps some are saying: "I know what Jesus said to do, but it doesn't make good sense. Why do we need to pray about something that is so obviously His will? It is His harvest. His followers are His laborers. If He wants them sent, why doesn't He just send them?"

I agree that it doesn't make sense unless you understand how God implements His will.

Two hundred years ago John Wesley said, "God does nothing but in answer to prayer." Wesley didn't give any further explanation of that statement, and I believed it for years before I understood it: God must wait until He is asked before He can do what He wants to do—not because He is powerless, but because of the way He has chosen to exercise His will.

Jesus was saying, "I want to send laborers, but you must pray. When you pray, I will send."

Ezekiel 36 contains a revelation of this very principle. Here the prophet, speaking in God's behalf, says to the nation of Israel: "I will take you from among the nations, gather you out of all countries, and bring you into your own land. Then I will sprinkle clean water on you, and you shall be clean; I will cleanse you from all your filthiness and from all your idols. I will give you a new heart and put a new spirit within you" (vv. 24-26). After re-emphasizing those words, God says, "I, the Lord, have spoken it, and I will do it" (v. 36). That is where most of us stop reading, but look at the next verse: "I will also let the house of Israel inquire of Me to do this for them." These things will God do, but not until He is asked.

The same principle is found in James: "You do not have because you do not ask" (4:2). We must pray; it is the only way God can legally intervene.

What I have tried to show in this teaching is that God operates by divine law and established principle; He exercises His will under strict rules. He has chosen to involve us in that process. And to me, that is exciting. We are not pawns on some great chessboard of life to be moved about by forces over which we have no control. We are involved. We are working together with God in the implementation of His holy will. Get these truths in your spirit and your attitude toward life will change. You can make a difference; you can set up the conditions under which things can be changed.

—B.J. Willhite was executive director of the Prayer Embassy in Washington, D.C.

Reprinted by permission Charisma Magazine and Strang Communications Company.

January 1989, Charisma

HOW TO FOLLOW GOD'S VOICE - IN INTERCESSION

MAKE ME AN INTERCESSOR

"And the smoke of the incense, which came with the prayers of the saints, ascended up before God out of the angel's hand" Revelation 8:4 KJV.

Make me an Intercessor,
    One who can really pray,
One of the Lord's Remembrancers
    By night as well as day.

Make me an Intercessor,
    In Spirit-touch with Thee,
And give the heavenly vision
    Praying through to victory.

Make me an Intercessor,
    Teach me how to prevail,
To stand my ground and still pray on.
    Though pow'rs of hell assail.

Make me an Intercessor,
    Sharing Thy death and life,
In prayer claiming for others,
    Victory in the strife.

Make me an Intercessor,
    Willing for deeper death,
Emptied, broken, then made anew,
    And filled with Living Breath.

Make me an Intercessor,
    Reveal this mighty thing,
The wondrous possibility
    Of paying back my King.

Make me an Intercessor,
    Hidden-unknown—set apart,
Thought little of by those around
    But satisfying thine heart.

—Paul Lee Tan is an author and preacher. His most popular book and software is *The Encyclopedia of 7700 Illustrations*. He formerly served as the Director of Asian Studies and Adjunct Professor at Dallas Theological Seminary and now has a ministry called Paul Lee Tan Prophetic Ministries.

Reprinted with permission from *Encyclopedia of 7700 Illustrations* by Paul Lee Tan, p. 1034

HOW TO FOLLOW GOD'S VOICE - IN INTERCESSION

SHAPING HISTORY AND OURSELVES

by Joy Dawson

Everyone has the opportunity to affect the course of history in his lifetime. Few realize this and take the opportunity.

Every time an intercessor for a nation is used to move God's hand, the greatest forces of power in the universe are mobilized and history is made. An intercessor constantly praying for the nations becomes one of the most powerful history-makers of his generation.

Intercession is praying as directed and being energized by the Holy Spirit for others. We cannot intercede for ourselves, but we can intervene between God and man, and, at times, satanic forces and man. Our greatest example of an intercessor is the Lord Jesus. Hebrews 7:25 says, "…He ever lives to make intercession for them" (NKJV). How little gratitude he receives for this faithful ministry on our behalf; and yet how much we owe Him for it!

One of the devil's most subtle and dangerous lies is that the ministry of intercession is mainly for old ladies or invalids who are unable to engage in other active service. Another lie is that it is for the favored few who are especially called to it. When we believe that, we fall for the third lie: that intercession is *not* the main responsibility of those called to leadership positions or active Christian service, and certainly is not for the average Christian.

The truth is that every child of God is called to be an intercessor. All our service for God will only be as effective as our prayer life for others is effective.

The more we pray for others, the less we will need to pray for ourselves. When we wait on God and ask Him to share His mind and heart with us concerning the person or people we are praying for, an exciting and rewarding thing takes place. He does just that. And as we speak those thoughts back to Him in faith, the unexpected happens. We get changed. In fact, nothing will change us more quickly and make us more like Him than intercessory prayer. Radical spiritual growth took place in my own life when I made serious prayer for others a part of my daily life.

The Bible tells us that intercession is uniquely a place where God gives revelation. In Jeremiah 33:3 God says, "Call to me and I will answer you, and will tell you great and hidden things which you have not known" (RSV). When we call to God on behalf of others, He promises to show us things. The first thing He shows us is how much He loves them, whether it's a person, an organization, a denomination, a race, an ethnic group or a nation. Revelation of people's deepest needs will always be given to loving intercessors because God thinks the most merciful, tolerant, loving and tender thoughts. In intercession God shares with us how He thinks and feels. Could anything change our heart attitudes toward people—and, in time, our mental habits—more quickly or more permanently?

Revelation of spiritual truths and future events are also given to intercessors. Moses, the greatest intercessor in the Old Testament, had the greatest revelation of the glory of God. Daniel, the man who had three prayer meetings per day, had remarkable revelation of present and future events. Anna, the prophetess who "…did not depart from the temple, worshipping with fasting and prayer night and day" (Luke 2:37, RSV), was given the revelation that the baby in Mary's arms was the promised Messiah. Cornelius and Peter made prayer a way of life on a consistent basis as recorded in Acts 10. Their reward was the startling revelation that the gospel was for the Gentiles as well as for the Jews.

June 1986 Charisma

God's character and His ways have not changed. It is with men and women who constantly intercede for others with clean hearts and pure motives that God shares His secrets today.

And included in this is the welfare of nations. In Psalms 2:8-9 God promises, upon our asking, to extend His kingdom among the nations: "Ask of me, and I will make the nations your heritage, and the ends of the earth your possession. You shall break them with a rod of iron, and dash them in pieces like a potter's vessel" (RSV).

In Isaiah 41:15 God promises to make us effective intercessors for that task: "Behold, I will make of you a threshing sledge, new, sharp, and having teeth; you shall thresh the mountains and crush them, and you shall make the hills like chaff" (RSV).

In Isaiah 61:11 God promises not only a harvest of righteousness, but a global bumper crop! "For as the earth brings forth its shoots, and as a garden causes what is sown in it to spring up, so the Lord God will cause righteousness and praise to spring forth before all the nations" (RSV).

Many desire to be intercessors.

Some determine to become intercessors.

Few discipline their lives and become intercessors

We may ask, "How will I ever become an effective intercessor?" The answer is the same as the angel gave to Mary: "The Holy Spirit shall come upon you." As we go regularly to the place of prayer, yield ourselves to God, ask for the on-coming of the Holy Spirit and believe Him to direct and energize us, He will. We cooperate by being obedient to His promptings. We learn to pray by praying!

If all our faculties were taken from us, except a sound mind and a beating heart, through the marvelous ministry of intercession we could still alter the course of history and hasten the Second Coming of the King of kings.

— Joy Dawson is an author, intercessor, and has been a missionary with Youth With a Mission International since 1970. She is a frequent speaker at leadership conferences around the world.

Reprinted by permission Charisma Magazine and Strang Communications Company.

June 1986, Charisma

HOW TO FOLLOW GOD'S VOICE—IN INTERCESSION

LESSON 2

THE NEED FOR INTERCESSION

MAIN PRINCIPLE

We need to realize the importance of intercessory prayer. It can change our life and the world around us.

HOW TO FOLLOW GOD'S VOICE - IN INTERCESSION

PASSIONATE PRAYER

by Mike Caulk

> "SOLITARY HOURS WITH GOD SHOULD BE FULL OF FERVENCY AND EARNESTNESS—NOT UNLIKE TWO LOVERS ALONE."

For this cause a man shall leave his father and mother, and shall cleave to his wife; and the two shall become one flesh."

Most wedding ceremonies I have witnessed or taken part in, even non-Christian ones, make some reference to this verse. However, few go on to the next sentence which says, "This mystery is great; but I am speaking with reference to Christ and the church" (Eph. 5:31,32). What does "for this cause" mean? What cause? What's the big mystery?

If you review the context of these two verses you quickly find the subject is husbands, wives, care, concern, and an intensely loving relationship between a man and a woman. The Holy Spirit, through Paul, is teaching us that God the Father wants us individually, and His entire church collectively, to see ourselves as married to His Son Jesus. We are not to be merely married in a legal or theological sense, but romantically attracted, emotionally bonded, really "in love" and sharing our lives together.

If this analogy is really an accurate picture of what God wants with us, then how grieved the Holy Spirit must be when we offer up detached, emotionally sterile and barren prayers. It must disappoint God when we come before Him only out of duty, guilt, or want; or when our time with Him is spent mumbling a few well-rehearsed charismatic theologies, listing a handful of personal needs, or relieving our conscience concerning our most recent sins. All too often this is done without giving any real affection or attention to the one who is supposed to be our genuine "first love."

If our life with Jesus is supposed to parallel that of two lovers, and I believe it is, then our prayer life should have an element of that same electric energy that surrounds the conversation of newlyweds. If you are not experiencing this kind of intensity in your conversations with the Lord, then consider the following five ingredients for passionate prayer.

BELIEF

In order to love we must first trust and respect the person we are loving. We must have a settled belief in them! Too often we attach or project human weakness to our mental image of God. This is nothing new. In Psalm 50:20,21, God says, "You sit and speak against your brother; you slander your own mother's son. These things you have done and I kept silent; you thought that I was just like you…" But God is not like us. Numbers 23:19 tells us that: "God is not a man, that He should lie, nor a son of man, that He should repent…"

It is vital that our emotions concerning God be firmly based on the unchanging scriptural revelation of God's true nature: His love, His mercy and His goodness. Paul wrote to the Roman believers "…the kindness of God leads you to repentance." To the saints in Galatia he said, "…in Christ Jesus neither circumcision nor uncircumcision means anything, but faith working through love." Real emotion in prayer comes out of a faith that is energized and fueled by admiration and affection, not by threats or religion!

DEVOTION

A natural outgrowth of belief is the second element in passionate prayer, devotion. By devotion I mean the commitment to forsake all others that is characteristic of anyone who has ever truly been in love. Solomon wrote about this kind of commitment saying, "There are sixty queens and eighty concubines, and maidens without number; but my dove, my perfect one, is unique…" No more shopping around checking out other possibilities. Your course is decided and your gaze is set on your special one and no other!

When real lovers go out to eat, what do they look at? They hardly notice the waiter—he is forced to return several times before they remember to look at the menu. They aren't admiring the décor. They aren't wondering if any of their friends are there. They are oblivious to all else. They are staring into each other's eyes, totally absorbed in one another. This is the way our communication with God should be. Just as a wife would never share her husband with another woman, God the Father wants us for Himself. There are to be no other gods before Him! He's not interested in deals, compromise, or half-hearted religious prayers.

SETTING

Another often-overlooked ingredient for real passionate prayer is a proper setting. You wouldn't go up to your wife in K-Mart, pull her close and kiss her intimately in the cash-only express line. There is a time and place for sharing that kind of affection with your mate. There is also a need to find the proper setting for your prayer time with Jesus. The Lord Himself addressed this by saying, "When you pray, go into your inner room, and when you have shut your door, pray to your Father who is in secret." Why the need for secrecy? Why such emphasis on isolation? Simply to eliminate distractions and make focusing on Jesus in an uninhibited manner as natural as possible. We also need to be isolated for our friends' sake. If we were to pray with friends who didn't share the same intensity in seeking Him, they would be uncomfortable and you would be grieved.

The right setting also involves creating the right atmosphere. As Christians we should be ready and able to pray anywhere, anytime, anyplace. Like Clark Kent we should stand poised and alert to transfigure instantly into a super-spiritual-intercessor at the first hint of need. But I am not talking about that kind of prayer. I am referring to our personal time with the Lord. That time of interaction requires soft lights and mood music. I believe God likes to communicate around good music too. David writes, "Thou art holy, O thou who art enthroned upon the praises of Israel," (Psalm 22:3).

If we have established a firm belief in His goodness and are devoted to Him alone, then out of us will flow a real desire for prayer.

DESIRE

Desire doesn't depend upon the one feeling the emotion, but comes from the one creating it! Ask any husband who is being affected by his wife's femininity. He is responding to her beauty. King David said, "One thing I have asked from the Lord, that I shall seek: that I may dwell in the house of the Lord all the days of my life, to behold the beauty of the Lord, and to meditate in His temple."

Notice the verse speaks of the beauty of the Lord. The Psalmist was not just looking at God in a general, vague kind of way. When I look at my wife, Missy, I look at specific things: her black hair, her pink lips, her deep brown eyes. I am almost always affected emotionally. It is impossible to really encounter Jesus and not be influenced, not just in a spiritual, ethereal sense, but in our emotions as well.

Again I want to quote David as he exhorts us to "…taste and see that the Lord is good…" (Psalm 34:8). When we experience this kind of biblical desire we will be motivated to new levels of expression with our Lord.

ABANDONMENT

Abandonment in prayer is the next level we experience. It is that state of spiritual vulnerability where we are free from the dread of being open about our feelings. There is a terror in being the first to say, "I love you." Ask anyone who has said it. There is an inherent fear in being really honest about our deepest emotions. Jesus said, "Truly I say to you, unless you are converted and become like children, you shall not enter the kingdom of heaven." Children are sometimes brutally frank and straightforward because they are totally emotionally free.

Unfortunately, as we grow up, we learn to bury and barricade our feelings, so when it comes to expressing our feelings to God, we flip the switch but nothing happens. In the opening book of the Bible, God says of the first two lovers, "They were both naked and were not ashamed." Jesus died to give us legal access into His presence. We can come with no fear, no inhibitions, nothing to hide. We can abandon all of our protective devices and lose ourselves in communion with Him.

This is what He wants. God is after just such an intimate relationship based on a solid belief in Fatherhood. This love will demand our fullest devotion and require us to take time to create the proper setting so that our desire for Him can cultivate and grow. As it does, we will find abandonment in His presence not only easy, but a delight and our prayers will reflect a real passion for God Himself!

— Mike Caulk was a preacher and history teacher. He pastored the Cornerstone Church in Lexington, Michigan, where he focused on prayer, praise and worship.

Reprinted with permission: Psalmist Magazine

HOW TO FOLLOW GOD'S VOICE - IN INTERCESSION

WHY PRAYER IS MY PRIORITY

by Tommy Barnett

SO MANY OF US NEGLECT DAILY TIME WITH GOD. I'VE LEARNED THAT PERSONAL TIME IN HIS PRESENCE IS NOT AN OPTION.

Nothing is accomplished except by prayer, penned John Wesley. The statement, once staggering to me, has been proved multiple times through the years of my life and ministry. As I have studied prayer, in all its vast dimensions, I now better understand Wesley's conviction: "Give me a hundred men, be it layman or clergy, who are not afraid of the devil, and their prayers will shake the gates of hell."

My early example of prayer came from my father, Hershel Barnett, who pastored 43 years in Kansas City. If ever there was a walking illustration of the Puritan saying, "When you pray, you move your feet," it was Dad. He built a great church by working tirelessly in the name of the Lord.

I remember as a child helping him fill out postcards after each Sunday evening service to send to all the visitors who had attended that day. It became a regular ritual for the two of us. No matter the lateness of the hour or the state of the weather, we would take an ever-growing stack of cards to the post office on those nights.

Before dropping them in the out-going mail containers, we'd pray over them. I can still feel the intensity of his prayer: "O God, bring people to church. Anoint these cards. Save souls." Only eternity will relate the impact of his faithfulness.

I remember walking with Dad around the church property that he believed God wanted him to have for growth. While we paced off the perimeters, he would ask God to give us the land, or use the current church land effectively, and touch people for Himself.

I also remember seeing Dad at the altar of his church in the afternoons, beseeching heaven for his congregation and city. Sometimes he would fall asleep while praying, only to awake to work again for the Father.

Most of his prayers were active prayers, prayers on the move. He was a goer, like myself. He would work and pray, possibly driven by Luke 18:1: "Men ought always to pray and not lose heart" (NKJV). His prayers accompanied him much like a companion.

In 1983 my life took a radical change when, unexpectedly, Dad graduated to his eternal reward. Only later did I learn that one of my heroes, Charles Spurgeon, wrote during his own final illness, "Grieve not when I die, for this was I born." But at the time I was unprepared for my father's death.

He had always told me he would never retire. On a Wednesday night he had preached a sermon; early the next morning he was "absent from the body and... present with the Lord" (see 2 Cor. 5:8).

I had become a preacher because he was one. He was my mentor and my friend. I loved and respected him, and each step of my life I reported to him and asked his advice. I wanted to be like him.

In retrospect, I will never doubt that I always believed the things that I preached. I knew and had appropriated the great truths of the gospel. Yet in many ways my ministry was based on my father's vision and his revelations from God.

Through introspection and struggle, I realized that my life was built on a solid foundation, but it was

Dad's foundation. Now that he was gone, I wondered whom I would turn to.

The anguish was relieved on one memorable day when the Word became flesh in my human experience: "When my heart is overwhelmed; lead me to the rock that is higher than I" (Ps. 61:2)—higher even than the unflappable pedestal that held my father. The Rock, Jesus, answered the overwhelmed heart in my innermost soul: "You can turn to Me…I have loved you with an everlasting love…I know the plans that I have for you."

While the days passed, I looked beyond Dad's revelation to find my own. Isaiah 6:1 described the end of my soul's search: "In the year that King Uzziah died, I saw the Lord." Uzziah was the prophet's friend and king; but when Isaiah lost his friend and leader, God stepped in as the God of all comfort.

> I USED TO BELIEVE THAT I EXPRESSED MY LOVE FOR GOD BY DOING GREAT EXPLOITS. NOW I UNDERSTAND THAT HE SEEKS MY DEVOTION MORE THAN MY SERVICE.

I began to see the Lord more clearly. It was as if everything that I had preached in my life instantly turned on with 10,000 watts of power. And suddenly prayer became mandatory—not the same on-the-go kind that accompanied Dad, but a driven desire for solitude, a longing to come apart, to "be still, and know that I am God" (Ps. 46:10). I established a specific time "apart" and found the best location for me was up on the mountain behind our church in Phoenix.

APPOINTMENT ON THE MOUNTAIN

I get up early to be with the Lord, even if services or flight schedules keep me up late at night. Usually He wakes me about 4:30 a.m. I go to the mountain, taking with me worldly cares and the care of my church. The Holy Spirit is my prayer partner. I run situations and concerns, vision and dreams through Him first. I say, "Holy Spirit, I need this or that," and He filters out what is not of God. Then He goes with me to the Father and often breaks into my conversations with God.

When words cannot communicate the needs I feel, it's as if the Holy Spirit takes those needs right from my being. As Phillips Brooks said, "Groanings that can't be uttered are often prayers that can't be refused."

In those times when I don't know how to relate or pray, I believe the Holy Spirit takes charge. He interprets to the Father: "This is what Tommy Barnett needs and what he doesn't need. This will help him and strengthen him. This will make him content, though he may not understand it now."

C.S. Lewis aptly stated that God answers prayer in one of two ways: "Yes" or "My grace is sufficient for you." I have learned from experience that "sufficient grace" for the "no" answers is readily available. Sincere disappointments often become God's appointments.

After all, He knows the end from the beginning. I can accept His answers because I'm convinced He is working to perfect that which concerns me, my family and the responsibilities He's given me in the body of Christ.

On the mountain, I pray for those who are my "sons" in the ministry. I pray for their personal concerns and for three specific things: first, that they will live pure and godly lives; second, that God will give them wisdom and strength to cope with the problems they face; and third, that God will keep them encouraged.

Yes, I pray for lots of encouragement. It is almost impossible for a defeated person to accomplish anything—so I ask God to keep them positive and encouraged through whatever trials they face. I believe there are great rewards for those ministries and ministers who stay holy before God, keep their motives right and promote unity.

TIME FOR SELAH

I've found that my prayers are best sent to heaven in solitude, in what I call my "Selah" time. The word *Selah* occurs 77 times in Scripture, connoting rest and the idea of a new sense of direction. I am convinced *selah* leads to active ministry that could not be achieved without that quiet time alone with the Father.

Selah is my time to pause and think, to focus on God, to thank Him for His fellowship and communication, to praise Him. It is also a time when I can respond to our Lord's need for love. It is easy to think about our own love needs and forget His; but it is one-sided loving if we don't answer His question. "Do you love me?" (John 21:7).

I used to believe I expressed my love for God by doing great exploits. Now I understand He wants me there for Him and seeks my devotion more than my service. Deuteronomy 32:9 underlines this: "The Lord's portion is His people." Holiness is His requirement—but our love is His joy and delight.

Much of the inward poverty I felt when my father died was relieved when I became quiet before God and listened. Praise God that I learned firsthand that the Lord is "my refuge and my fortress; my God, in Him I will trust" (Ps. 9:12).

The basis of my security became the character of Father God. My heart was fixed on Him, and firsthand revelation from God Himself became the difference between mediocrity and success in my life ministry.

As ministers we are drawn into solitude and prayer in three ways. First, God draws us when we are open-hearted and desire the mind of Christ in us. Even as God drew Elijah to the Brook Cherith, He desires to bring us to Himself.

Second, circumstances drive us to solitude—like when my dad died, or when it appears the foundations of our faith are failing. The financial stresses of the explosive outreaches at our Los Angeles International Church are monumental. But you know what? They drive me right into the arms of the Father via the Holy Spirit. And there they rest, and I rest, holding fast to my confidence in the one who does all things well.

Third, we arrange our appointed times of solitude with God. The Bible instructs us to study to be quiet (see 1Thess. 4:11). Another translator notes that we are to concentrate on being quiet, learning to accept the discipline that produces *selah*.

A.W. Tozer once wrote, "All things else being equal, our prayers are only as powerful as our lives. In the long pull we pray only as well as we live." I've discovered it is not sufficient simply to try to take time for quietness but that I must, with all diligence, make time. Whatever keeps me from prayer, solitude and the Bible, however good it appears, is my enemy if I am to be God's devoted friend and follower.

In fact, the busier I am the more I go into *selah*. It alone prepares me for the vastness of the task before me. Even through long, arduous days of pastoring a church of 10,000 in Phoenix, co-pastoring and administrating another in Los Angeles, being a pastor to pastors, and maintaining an unforgiving travel schedule, *selah* time keeps it all in perspective.

I am alarmed for pastors and Christians who crowd out the Lord with the tyranny of the urgent, who treat prayer casually. What is more urgent than being with Him, our maker, creator and sustainer?

If you are distressed by the problems, frustrations and anxiety with which you live and minister, I implore you to "come apart." Battles are part of the journey we're on; the armor for the battles is faith, obedience and prevailing prayer.

At some point still ahead, when I step through the gates of heaven with an eternity before me to worship the Lord, I anticipate seeing Dad and all the souls won with our prayers and dedicated service. And perhaps someplace close to the Eastern Gate I'll be able to tell John Wesley: "You were right. I found it true: *Nothing is accomplished except by prayer.*"

— Tommy Barnett is an author, pastor and a chancellor of Southeastern University. He currently is the senior pastor of Phoenix First Assembly of God in Phoenix, Arizona. He has authored several books, including *Multiplication, Hidden Power, and Enlarge Your Circle of Love.*

Reprinted with permission from Ministry Today, November/December 1996. Copyright Strang Communications Co., USA. All rights reserved.

HOW TO FOLLOW GOD'S VOICE - IN INTERCESSION

THE LANGUAGE OF INTERCESSION

by Cindy Jacobs

A BETTER UNDERSTANDING OF THE TERMS WE USE IN PRAYER WILL HELP US INTERCEDE WITH GREATER CLARITY AND AUTHORITY.

Sunday morning—what an exciting time for a new believer! After taking her seat, Susan scans the weekly announcements, stopping at the line that says: "Ladies' Intercession Group Tuesday Morning! Come and join in a time of prayer for our church and our city."

Susan feels a stirring in her heart. Could she pray for others' needs? She puts the announcement in her purse, eager for Tuesday to arrive.

Tuesday morning she arrives at church, takes her son to the nursery and slips into the room where the prayer meeting is being held. As the prayer leader calls the group to order, Susan waits eagerly for instructions.

But what she hears leaves her in confusion: "A serious stronghold is coming against our church. This yoke is strangling the church, so we need to bind the enemy's control. Let's pray the prayer of agreement, loose the will of God and intercede until we have prayed this through."

By the time the leader begins praying, Susan is in a panic. *What makes me think that I can be an intercessor? She thinks. I didn't even understand half of what the leader was saying.*

This scenario is not uncommon in churches today. Eventually, if Susan doesn't give up, she will break the "code" of intercession and become familiar with phrases such as "prayer of agreement."

But without proper training, Susan—like many other aspiring intercessors—will have only a superficial understanding of the biblical meaning of the words used in prayer. All too often in this case, the language of intercession becomes jargon—and misunderstanding and confusion are the result.

But God is not the author of confusion. Rather, He wants us to have a clear definition of these terms, so we can pray with greater clarity and authority. Having a better understanding of a few basic terms should help us appropriate the language of intercession to resist satanic powers and see God's purposes accomplished in human affairs.

STRONGHOLDS

The weapons of our warfare are not carnal but mighty in God for pulling down strongholds (2 Cor. 10:4).

Strongholds are fortified places Satan builds to exalt himself against the knowledge and plans of God. Edgardo Silvoso of Harvest Evangelism gives this definition of a stronghold: "A stronghold is a mind-set impregnated with hopelessness that causes the believer to accept as unchangeable something that he or she knows is contrary to the will of God."

In his book *Overcoming the Dominion of Darkness* (Revell), Pastor Gary Kinnaman identifies three types of strongholds:

- **Personal strongholds.** Kinnaman says these are evil or sinful things that Satan builds to influence a person's thoughts, feelings, attitudes and behavior patterns.
- **Ideological strongholds.** These strongholds, according to Kinnaman, concern Satan's dominance of the world view through philosophies that influence culture and society. Charles Dar-

October 1993, Charisma

win's theory of natural selection, which opposes biblical creation, could be considered an ideological stronghold.

These strongholds are portrayed in 2 Corinthians 10: "Casting down arguments and every high thing that exalts itself against the knowledge of God, [we bring] every thought into captivity to the obedience of Christ" (v. 5).

- **Territorial strongholds.** Kinnaman says these represent the hierarchy of dark beings assigned by Satan to influence and control nations, communities and even families. Certain demonic forces mass to different regions to fortify particular types of evil. Certain cities will be strongholds of idolatry, sensual sin or certain kinds of religious spirits.

The ancient city of Pergamos could be considered a territorial stronghold. In Revelation 2:13, the city is described as "where Satan's throne is" and "where Satan dwells." According to *Unger's Bible Dictionary:* "The city was greatly addicted to idolatry, and its grove…was filled with statues and altars."

As the founder of Generals of Intercession, a ministry dedicated to prayer and spiritual warfare, I've had many opportunities to witness the effects of tearing down strongholds. One of the most dramatic incidents occurred in September 1990 when Generals of Intercession met with local intercessors in the city of Mar del Plata, Argentina.

The intercessors discerned four major territorial spirits ruling over Mar del Plata and a "strong man" ruler who reigned over the four. After we fasted and prayed, we gathered about 300 people to join us in prayer. As the cathedral bells chimed 4 p.m., we began praying against the ruling spirit—witchcraft.

After our time of prayer, one of the local pastors received a phone call asking what we'd been doing at 4 p.m. The reason for the caller's curiosity: One of the witches who had been invoking curses against the city's pastors dropped dead—right at 4 p.m.

We were stunned. Although saddened that the woman had died, we recognized that God was sending a clear message of judgment upon witchcraft.

When Satan's strongholds are pulled down, his kingdom cannot stand: "When a strong man, fully armed, guards his own palace, his goods are in peace. But when a stronger than he comes upon him and overcomes him, he takes from him all his armor in which he trusted, and divides his spoils" (Luke 11:21-22).

PRAYING IN AGREEMENT
If two of you agree on earth concerning anything that they ask, it will be done for them by My Father in heaven (Matt. 18:19).

The Greek word translated "agree" in Matthew 18:19 means "to be harmonious or symphonize." A symphony, then, can help illustrate what it means to agree in prayer.

When a symphony plays, many instruments perform, each adding its own quality to the blend heard by the composer. In a similar manner, God uses many types of prayers and intercessors to orchestrate His divine melody of prayer.

Praying in agreement also might be likened to filling a bottle of water. One person may pour in 20 percent, another 30 percent, another 10 percent, and so on until the bottle is full. When the bottle is filled to the brim, agreement is complete and the task is finished. Though some people may feel their prayers don't amount to much, those prayers may be the last drops needed to fill the bottle.

When the Berlin Wall fell in November 1989, people everywhere expressed their surprise at this turn of events. But for some people—God's intercessors—the wall's demise was not unexpected because they had prayed in agreement for that to take place.

Prayer leader Dick Eastman, for example, has shared his memories of a bitterly cold day when he placed his hands on the Berlin Wall and prayed with expectancy that it would come down. Another prayer leader, Gwen Shaw of the End-Time Handmaidens, tells how she stood before the wall in 1987 and led a group of intercessors to pray for its collapse. More than a year before the wall came down, as I prayed for a missionary to East Germany, I was surprised to hear these prophetic words come out of my mouth: "The wall will literally be disassembled piece by piece and brick by brick, and I will let My people go." These are examples of people praying in agreement.

AGREEING TOGETHER
Here are two questions I'm often asked about the prayer of agreement:
- **How many people does it take to pray until a certain need is met?** Several factors determine the number that God will call to pray:
1. What kind of stronghold are you dealing with? The stronger the resistance or higher the territorial power, the more people will be required to break the stronghold.

October 1993, Charisma

2. What level of authority does the person praying have in the Spirit? A certain authority comes forth when an intercessor believes wholeheartedly that God will move in response to his or her prayer, and God's enemies know they're in trouble when this authority rings out in a prayer meeting.
3. Has fasting been coupled with prayer? Fasting multiplies the effect of prayer and will touch things that prayer alone will not affect.

- **How do I go about agreeing in prayer with someone who comes to me with a need?** When joining someone in a prayer of agreement, you should consider these points:

1. How are you to pray concerning a need? You may be praying, for instance, for a sick relative and believing God for a miracle. But the person with whom you're praying may be asking the Lord only to comfort that person. When people call me with a request, I typically ask, "How has the Lord led you to pray in this situation?"
2. If I don't agree with the way others are praying, rather than tell them so, I sometimes mention the way that I feel led to pray. If they agree with that approach, I pray with them right away.
3. Has the Holy Spirit given you any Scripture verses concerning this need? If God has given you some revelation from His Word, are you in unity with the other person about it?
4. If you and the other person are in agreement, you might pray something like this: "Father, I agree with what my friend has asked You for. Your word declares: 'If two of you agree on earth concerning anything that they ask, it will be done for them.' Now, according to Your word, I thank You for answered prayer."

BINDING AND LOOSING

Whatever you bind on earth will be bound in heaven, and whatever you loose on earth will be loosed in heaven (Matthew 18:18).

According to Gary Kinnaman, the concept of "binding and loosing" did not originate with Jesus, but was a frequent expression of first-century Jewish rabbinical dialect. To the Jewish rabbis, "binding and loosing" meant simply "prohibiting and permitting"—that is, "establishing." These religious authorities, Kinnaman says, exercised the right to establish guidelines for religious practice and social interaction.

But binding and loosing also refers to supernatural control. In Luke 13:13-16, Jesus used the same root words to explain his healing of a woman afflicted by Satan: "Ought not this woman, being a daughter of Abraham, whom Satan has *bound*...for eighteen years, be *loosed* from this bond" (emphasis mine).

Through this encounter, Jesus was showing the Jewish leaders that binding and loosing has a supernatural side. Notice that He said specifically that it was Satan who had bound the woman.

Jesus told his disciples: "Whatever you bind on earth will be bound in heaven, and whatever you loose on earth will be loosed in heaven" (Matt. 18:18). I believe He was giving them authority in heavenly places, the unseen realm where all things on the earth can be bound or loosed—disallowed or allowed.

NEGATIVE BINDING

My hometown of Weatherford, Texas, furnishes a helpful illustration for negative binding. When Weatherford has its annual rodeo, cowboys come from all over to compete in activities such as roping and bronco-busting. The event that best depicts binding is the calf-roping and tying. A cowboy chases and ropes a calf from his horse, pulls it to the ground and ties the calf's legs together so it cannot move; this done, the cowboy throws up his hands in a gesture of victory.

This is the picture of what happens in the spiritual realm when we pray to tie (or bind) Satan from having anything to do with a given situation. How does this work?

As intercessors, we become aware of a certain situation in which Satan is trying to cause problems, and we go to our place of prayer. Using the illustration of the cowboy, we take our rope, which is the Word of God, and ride the vehicle of prayer out to stop the work of Satan.

Then, we release our rope by speaking the Word of God: "Satan, I bind (or tie) you in the name of Jesus! The Word says that whatever I bind on earth will be bound in heaven, and whatever I loose on earth will be loosed in heaven. In the name of Jesus, I forbid you to cause any more strife!"

Some situations require more than one person to do the binding, and the weapon of binding needs to be coupled with the prayer of agreement. Each person who prays throws a rope until the prayers completely bind the attack of Satan.

Because distance doesn't exist in the realm of the Spirit, the weapon of binding is just as effective long-distance as it is close-range. So we don't have to be with the person being attacked for the prayer of binding to stop the enemy's work.

October 1993, Charisma

POSITIVE BINDING

Positive binding occurs when we speak the Word of God over a given situation, making the enemy weaker until he is unable to resist God's purposes. The most powerful example of positive binding was given by Jesus Himself when He battled Satan in the wilderness (see Luke 4:1-13). Jesus spoke God's Word over and over against the enemy until his power to tempt Jesus was broken. From this example, notice that positive binding doesn't always stop the enemy immediately. Many times the struggle will be long and intense.

How do we put positive binding in practice?

If we are praying for a church in disunity, for example, we would quote Psalm 133:1: "Behold, how good and how pleasant it is for brethren to dwell together in unity!" If we are praying over a loved one who needs the Lord, we could quote Luke 19:10: "The Son of Man has come to seek and to save that which was lost." As we make God's Word binding in the situation, it will combat evil works and anything that exalts itself against the knowledge of God.

LOOSING

God uses our prayers to carry out His will. Loosing in prayer releases or permits God's will to enter and change a situation. Let me give you an example:

The intercessory team at the Lausanne II Congress on World Evangelization, held in July 1989 in Manila, was gathered for a prayer watch. While we were praying, a special request came through for Bruce Olson, a missionary to the Motilone Indians in Colombia. Bruce had been captured nine months before by communist guerrillas, who had now issued a statement that he would be executed within the week.

Each intercessor sensed that the Lord wanted to stop the guerrillas and use Bruce further in ministry. The enemy had to be halted and the captive loosed.

It was Wednesday afternoon, July 12. Joy Dawson was asked to lead the group in prayer for Bruce. Joy—a petite, lovely, former New Zealander—is a general in God's army with a no-nonsense approach to intercession.

Before praying anything, Joy stood and waited on God. She then started by praising and thanking God for His sovereign and complete control over the situation. Next, she committed Bruce into God's hands, declaring her trust that he was acting on Bruce's behalf to bring the maximum glory to the Lord Jesus. After that, she asked God to dispense ministering angels to Bruce and keep his mind in perfect peace.

The intercessors were in agreement as Joy began to war against satanic forces with the authority that came from knowing she had been given a right to do so by the heavenly Commander in Chief. She wielded the sword of the Spirit boldly by binding the forces of darkness operating against Bruce Olson. Declaring Jesus' shed blood as the grounds for Satan's total defeat, she exercised faith in the Lord's name to loose Bruce from all the enemy's power and schemes. She concluded by praising God that His almighty power and plans were in operation.

I did not hear the story of Bruce Olson's release until after returning home from Manila, when I read the report in *Charisma* Magazine. As I read the article, I was deeply touched to find that his release occurred exactly one week after the intercession that took place in Manila. Although many people had been praying for his release, I believe the intercession on that particular day helped to loose a captive to fulfill God's destiny for his life.

A loosing prayer can have the following effects:
1. It can bring about the release of a captive, as in the case of Bruce Olson.
2. It can release a person from sickness or disease, as in the case of the woman whom Satan had bound with an infirmity.
3. It can loose or declare the will of God to be done in a certain situation.
4. It can loose God to move in and change situations.

BREAKING A YOKE

The yoke shall be destroyed because of the anointing (Is. 10:27, KJV).

In biblical times, a pair of oxen was joined together at the neck by a wooden frame called a yoke. A strong or lead ox would take the larger side and the younger, weaker ox the opposite side. As they pulled, the weaker ox had to keep in step with the stronger ox.

When we are in the yoke with Christ, the burden is light because He is the stronger one pulling the weight (see Matt. 11:29-30). But Satan has counterfeited this principle to put heavy yokes on people to bring them into bondage to sin, occultic oppressions and wrong relationships.

The Bible is clear that we are not to be yoked to any evil influence: "Do not be unequally yoked together with unbelievers. For what fellowship has righteousness with lawlessness?.... And what accord has Christ with Belial?" (2 Cor. 6:14-15).

October 1993, Charisma

How should we pray for someone who is enslaved by Satan's yoke? There are several effective weapons:

- **Receive the anointing.** The anointing of the Holy Spirit is a mighty weapon in breaking yokes (see Is. 10:27). The Spirit will move through us in powerful intercession and tear apart the yokes of Satan.
- **Fast.** In Isaiah 58:6, we read: "Is this not the fast that I have chosen: to loose the bonds of wickedness, to undo the heavy burdens, to let the oppressed go free, and that you break every yoke?
- **Bind the power of the evil one.** In the authority of Christ, command Satan and his forces to stop blinding the individual's eyes to the glorious light of the gospel (see 2 Cor. 4:4). Forbid evil spirits from holding him or her in their grasp.
- **Pray for the power of evil to be broken.** Pray authoritatively against the power of sin, legalism and occultic practices and so on in the person's life. Pray for any evil tie to be broken and for the people involved to be loosed from any wrong relationship.
- **Praise the Lord.** According to Psalms 146 and 149, praise is a catalyst for setting captives free and binding evil rulers with chains

STANDING IN THE GAP

We are in a holy war for the souls of men and women. We are wrestling in the heavenly places against an enemy who is ruthless in his desire to steal, kill and destroy. And his greatest weapon is the passivity of believers.

Now, as in the past, God is looking for people "who would make a wall, and stand in the gap before Me on behalf of the land" (Ezek. 22:30). The wall here is not made of stones, but of faithful intercessors united in their efforts to bridge "the gap" between a lost world and a loving God.

If we fail to respond at this critical time—if we neglect to train and equip ourselves as intercessors—we will fail to help fulfill God's plans for the nations to come to the glorious light of the gospel.

I pray that God will not say to this generation as He said to Ezekiel's: "I sought for someone… who would stand in the gap…but I found no one."

— Cindy Jacobs is a respected prophet who travels the world ministering not only to crowds of people, but also to heads of nations. Cindy has authored several books, including *Possessing the Gates of the Enemy, The Voice of God and The Power of Persistent Prayer.* Cindy loves to travel and speak, but one of her favorite pastimes is spending time with her husband Mike, two grown children and their adorable grandchildren.

Reprinted by permission Chrisma Magazine and Strang Communications and Company.

October 1993, Charisma

LESSON 3

JESUS, OUR INTERCESSOR

MAIN PRINCIPLE

Knowing, believing and abiding in the Word of God, imparts to us an intercessory prayer life parallel to Christ's—of asking and receiving all for the glory of God. Successful intercessory prayer is the fruit of a surrendered life of abiding in Christ.

HOW TO FOLLOW GOD'S VOICE - IN INTERCESSION

FOCUS ON JESUS

by Barbara Shull

Have you ever reached a point of discouragement in your prayers for someone or in your daily walk with God? Have you ever felt so entangled in sin or so encumbered with burdens that you felt you couldn't pray or continue in fellowship with the Lord?

God has some good advice for the times we get into such predicaments. Better yet, He tells us how to prevent them. "Let us also lay aside every encumbrance, and the sin which so easily entangles us, and let us run with endurance the race that is set before us, fixing our eyes on Jesus, the author and perfecter of faith" (Heb. 12:1-2 NASB). The thing to learn is that God will enable you to lay aside your burdens and to run with endurance only as you fix your eyes steadfastly on Jesus! Don't focus on problems!

There will be many obstacles in the way as you run your race. Satan is one of them. You can be so intent upon avoiding him that you run right into him, like trying to miss a telephone pole while learning to ride a bicycle and steering straight for it! The same thing can be true of a bad habit. If you focus your attention on it, feverishly trying to change it, it may even become worse.

God's promise is that if you look to Jesus and concentrate on Him you will become like Him. Our well-being hinges on our attention being focused on Jesus. He tells us this when we read, "The light of the body is the eye: if therefore thine eye be single, thy whole body shall be full of light" (Matt. 6:22 KJV).

The Scriptures repeatedly remind us of the importance of having your focus on Him. We are told of blessings as we do and dangerous consequences when we don't.

When the eyes of your heart and mind are set on Him alone, God promises salvation in full from all things that hinder wholeness and health (Isa. 45:22), provision (Ps. 81:13,16), guidance (2 Chron. 20:12-17), mercy (Ps. 123:1-2), life (Rom. 8:5-6), joy (Ps. 16:8-9), perfect peace (Isa. 26:3), and victory over our enemies (Ps. 81:13-14), among other things. On the other hand, he warns that a double-minded man must not presume he will receive anything from the Lord (James 1:6-8).

God desires not only a single eye but also a single ear, a single heart, and a single mind. These physical terms are actually symbols of a spiritual attitude and sensitivity toward the Spirit of God. While the singleness is primarily a matter of attitude, God also enables you to visualize Him, using your imagination. Mental pictures of Him should not focus as much on his physical features as on His personality and character: His faithfulness, His love, His power, etc.

How important it is to let the Holy Spirit search your innermost being and reveal the true objects of your attention. He is the one who can show you if your mind is set on things above or on things of earth (Col. 3:1-2).

God enables you to have a single eye as you walk with Christ. He often uses the trials and difficulties which you encounter for the purpose of strengthening your focus on Him.

Such a single focus is absolutely essential for effective praying. If, as an intercessor, you walk with your eyes fixed on Jesus, whenever you sense someone's deep need or hear some tragic news, you will pray for them in peace, rejoicing that you know exactly who is the answer to the problem. Looking to Jesus, you can immediately ask for His divine intervention. David knew this truth: "He shall not be afraid of evil tidings; his heart is firmly fixed trusting…in the Lord" (Ps. 112:7 TAB).

Being tuned into God alone as you pray gives you the ability to receive specific instructions from God. There are no formulas for prayers just as there are no formulas to receive answers. God chooses to work uniquely in each situation. Since we can be sure that those prayers which are prayed according to His will are heard and answered (1 John 5:14-15), we should look to the Father to find out how He wants us to pray or intercede for each particular concern. Sometimes you will sense, in a general way, how and what you are to pray. Other times God will reveal His will very specifically and exactly.

Jesus, our chief example, while walking this earth, had His eye fixed on His Father in heaven. He Himself said, "Truly, truly I say to you, the Son can do nothing of Himself, unless it is something He sees the Father doing" (John 5:19 NASB). Even though Jesus was compassionate and sensitive to the manifold needs of the people around Him, He did not focus His full attention on them. In fact, He didn't make a move to meet their needs until He received instruction from His Father.

Still another reason why it is essential for you as an intercessor to have a single eye is because part of your job is to bear burdens. By keeping tuned into Jesus, you can discern which burdens He intends you to bear and which He doesn't.

When you are burdened by cares, whether your own or another's, it is quite easy for your human compassion and emotions to take over. In fact, it is even possible to experience psychic or other soul-inspired sensations. To avoid this you should have your heart and mind fully centered on the Lord, not on the person in need, not on the situation, not on the enemy, not on yourself, not on your prayers, nor on any manifestations: only on Jesus.

God does not intend for us to feel His heartbreak constantly or to carry heavy burdens. Only occasionally does he share one. When He does, he expects the intercessor to pray through to a release of faith. When this is done and the heartbreaking burden has been given back to Him, peace, and often the joy of the Lord, follows, leaving the intercessor once again burden-free, ready to run with endurance, eyes fixed on Jesus.

—Excerpted from Barbara Shull's book, *How to Become a Skilled Intercessor*, published by Women's Aglow Fellowship, Lynwood WA (now Aglow International, Edmonds WA).

Reprinted with permission: Women's Aglow Fellowship.

HOW TO FOLLOW GOD'S VOICE - IN INTERCESSION

THE THREE PURPOSES FOR INTERCESSORY PRAYER (Part 1)

by Ralph Mahoney

We have two intercessors at work on our behalf: the Holy Spirit, and the Lord Jesus Christ. *"It is* Christ who died, and furthermore is also risen, who is even at the right hand of God, who also makes intercession for us" (Rom. 8:34). Romans 8:26 also tells us, "The Spirit also helps in our weaknesses. For we do not know what we should pray for as we ought, but the Spirit Himself makes intercession for us."

It is my conviction that everything the Lord Jesus Christ does on earth, he does through His body, the Church. He is not disconnected from us, but we, as members of His body, express His ministry in the world. Only when we lay hands on the sick is there an opportunity for healing. Only when we take the Gospel to others do they have an opportunity to believe.

Of course, there are exceptions; but usually, God depends upon the members of His body to implement His will and His ministry on earth. Those who have joined the family of God are to join the Spirit and the Son in making intercession.

According to Scripture, the believers' intercessory prayer has three purposes: 1) to stand in the gap on behalf of others, 2) to birth the purposes of God through the Church, and 3) to provide protection for the work and the workers of God.

STANDING IN THE GAP

When Job was going through his tribulation, he longed for someone to connect him with God. "Oh, that one might plead for a man with God, as a man *pleads* for his neighbor!" (Job 16:21). That's what intercession is all about: pleading the cause of another before God.

Before we can stand in the gap, we need to understand what created the gap in the first place. Most ancient cities were secured with walls for one important reason: There were bandits who roamed throughout the countryside, and people who did not live within the walls of a city were vulnerable to attack. If there was even one breach in the wall—stones knocked out or the wall was weak and crumbling in one spot—the enemy could come into the city to pillage and destroy.

> THOSE WHO HAVE JOINED THE FAMILY OF GOD ARE TO JOIN THE SPIRIT AND THE SON IN MAKING INTERCESSION.

Isaiah 30:12,13 describes what causes a breach in the wall of people's lives, in the walls of churches and in the wall of nations: "Thus says the Holy One of Israel: 'Because you despise this word, and trust in oppression and perversity, and rely on them, therefore this iniquity shall be to you like a breach ready to fall, a bulge in a high wall, whose breaking comes suddenly, in an instant.'"

The prophet is saying that sin causes a breach or a bulge in the wall, which causes the wall to collapse. And when the wall falls, we're wide open to the attack of the enemy. Sin makes an opening for the enemy to come in to kill, steal and destroy.

In the book of Revelation, Christ's message to the first of the seven churches of Asia was, "I have *this* against you, that you have left your first love" (Rev. 2:4). We leave our first love by choice. We choose to allow our love for the Lord to grow cold.

The call of Christ to the Church at Ephesus is this: "Remember therefore from where you have fallen; repent and do the first works" (Rev. 2:5). In leaving their first love, they had allowed a breach to form in the wall. Christ was warning the Ephesians that there would be serious consequences if the breach was not repaired: "I will come to you quickly and remove your lampstand from its place—unless you repent" (Rev. 2:5). Without the lampstand—the gifts of the Holy Spirit—believers are powerless against the works of darkness.

It has happened in the Church again and again: Believers grow cold in their love for the Lord, the lampstand is removed, and they're left powerless. The enemy comes in because they have no power to resist, no authority over devils, no power to heal the sick. The rituals and the forms are perpetuated, but there's no power (see II Tim. 3:1-5). Sin creates a breach in the wall.

The prophet Ezekiel understood this principle. God showed him there was a huge breach in the wall because of the sin of the nation. God saw that all of Israel—the princes, the prophets, the priests and the people—had become oppressors of the orphans and widows, slanderers, sexual perverts, filled with greed, idolaters and even murders. The Lord told Ezekiel, "The house of Israel has become dross to Me....Yes, I will gather you and blow on you with the fire of My wrath" (Ezek. 22:18,21).

God mentions that the princes of Israel were involved (Ezek. 22:6,27). He also talks about the prophets and the priests (vs. 25,26,28). Backsliding usually has its source in the leadership. As long as the leaders stay faithful to God, the people follow. But when the leadership becomes unfaithful, the people also follow.

Through their fear and unbelief, 10 men kept 2.5 million Israelites wandering in the wilderness for 40 years. Only Joshua and Caleb came back with a good report.

In the United States today, many church leaders are spineless! They will not stand up and make a distinction between holy and profane, clean and unclean. Most don't have the courage to call abortion what it actually is: murder of an unborn child. We have churches in San Francisco that openly promote homosexuality with their membership almost 100% homosexual. Of course we should reach out to them in love and try to turn them from their way; but as long as we don't make any distinction between the holy and the profane, there will never be a turning from it.

Because the priests of Ezekiel's day did not make any distinction between the holy and the profane, the unclean and the clean, God's judgments hung over the nation. God said, "I sought for a man among them who would make a wall, and stand in the gap before Me on behalf of the land, that I should not destroy it; but I found no one" (Ezek. 22:30). The sin of the leadership had created a bulge in the wall, and it had fallen. God was looking for an intercessor, someone who would stand in the gap before Him, but He found no one. I've often wondered if that's the condition the Lord finds when He searches for intercessors in American churches.

In Ezekiel 9:4, the Lord said, "Go through the midst of the city, through the midst of Jerusalem, and put a mark on the foreheads of the men who sigh and cry over all the abominations that are done within it." When judgment came on Jerusalem, only those with the mark on their forehead were spared. All the rest came under judgment and went into captivity.

We're living under the threat of judgment in our own nation today, and God is looking for those who will stand in the gap as intercessors. I believe that when judgment comes, each of us will have one of two marks: the mark of the intercessor or the mark of the beast. It behooves us to understand the wonderful privilege that is ours of entering into Christ's intercessory ministry, standing in the gap before God, pleading for our nation, our city, our church and our own family.

When we see the enemy moving in, what should we do? Stand in the gap; plead for them. Do not surrender them to the enemy's plans. As we stand in the gap, the revelation of God may begin to flow, giving us the practical action required to implement God's program of recovery and salvation for them.

Paul tells us in II Corinthians 5:18,19 that we have both the Word and ministry of reconciliation to reconcile men to God. Part of that ministry is fulfilled when we stand in the gap for our friends, children, relatives, institutions, churches, cities, states, nations—even our enemies. We can stand in the gap as intercessors, and the Lord is seeking men and women who will do that.

Psalm 106:23 says this: "He (God) said that He would destroy them, had not Moses His chosen one stood before Him in the breach, to turn away His wrath, lest He destroy *them*." Jesus said a good shepherd will lay down his life for the sheep (Jn. 10:11). Moses proved himself a true shepherd. God was offering to blot out the people and start over with Moses. But he stood before God and said, "Lord, if you wipe them out, blot me out with them. If you're going to blot their names out, just blot mine out, too. I'm not going to be separated from them. Their destiny is my destiny." (See Ex. 32:10,33.) What a compassionate leader!

Moses turned away God's wrath by standing in the gap. The nation was spared. Next, the Lord said He would be willing to send an angel to help wipe out their enemies. But Moses replied, "If Your Presence does not go *with us*, do not bring us up from here. For how then will it be known that Your people and I have found grace in your sight, except You go with us?" (Ex. 33:15,16). That's what we need more than anything else: the presence and the power of God.

Daniel lived in the time that Jeremiah's prophecy had been fulfilled. Jeremiah had prophesied that Jerusalem would remain in ruins while Israel experienced a 70-year captivity. By reading the prophecy, Daniel recognized the 70 years were over and understood it was time for the Israelites to go back to Jerusalem and to believe for restoration of the temple and the city.

So Daniel stood in the gap for Israel: "I set my face toward the Lord God to make request by fasting, sackcloth, and ashes. ...'We have sinned and committed iniquity; we have done wickedly and rebelled, even by departing from Your precepts and Your judgments. ... Yes, all Israel has transgressed Your law, and has departed so as not to obey Your voice; therefore the curse and the oath written in the Law of Moses the servant of God have been poured out on us, because we have sinned against Him'" (Dan. 9:3,5,11).

Daniel confessed the sin of the whole nation to the Lord! We need to understand the principle involved in standing in the gap. The United States certainly has a huge breach in its wall.

The Bible says to pray for "all who are in authority" (I Tim. 2:2), and we think that means to pray a blessing on them. I pray for leaders this way: "Lord, bring down the wicked and exalt the righteous." We are to love our enemies, and we are not to render evil for evil (1 Pet. 3:9).

But there's a distinction between our enemies and God's enemies, between those who make mistakes in relating to us and those who are truly wicked. We don't want to pray blessing on the wicked. We want to pray, "God, exalt the righteous, and bring down the wicked." That's part of our intercessory ministry.

—Adapted form a message given at CFNI in Dallas.

Ralph Mahoney was an author and the founder of World Map (a Missions organization that focuses on the Great Commission and equipping leaders). His most famous book, The Shepherd's Staff, has encouraged millions of pastors and is in 18 different languages.

Reprinted by permission: Christ for the Nations. CFNI, P.O. Box 769000, Dallas, TX 75376-9000, 800-933-2364

HOW TO FOLLOW GOD'S VOICE - INTERCESSION

PRAYER THAT IS PLEASING TO THE LORD

by David Wilkerson

I want to talk to you today about a kind of prayer that is most pleasing to the Lord. You see, not all of our praying blesses the heart of God. Yet, with the help of the Holy Spirit, I trust that what I share with you here will change the way you pray—from now until Jesus comes!

I have no intention of complicating prayer. It has been made too complicated already by well-intentioned teachers who have turned it into formulas, strategies and theatrics. Some Christians literally put on combat boots and uniforms to dress the part of "prayer warriors." Others attend prayer meetings where they are given "prayer guides," booklets that tell them how to fill up the hours they'll be there.

I am not condemning any of this. But I would like to show you the kind of praying I believe pleases the Lord most. Actually, the kind of prayer that most pleases God is very simple and easy to understand. It is so simple, in fact, a little child can pray in a way that pleases Him.

Let me begin by saying, I believe most Christians want to pray. At one time in our walk with the Lord, we all prayed with some consistency. But after a while, many believers quit. And now they are convicted by their prayerlessness.

The disciples said to Jesus, "...Lord, teach us to pray..." (Luke 11:1). They would not have asked unless they had wanted to learn. And I believe that most who are reading this message would love to be faithful in prayer—but they don't know how. The problem is, they simply don't understand the purpose of prayer. And until they grasp this vital purpose, they will never be able to maintain a fulfilled, meaningful life of prayer.

Many Christians pray only out of a sense of obligation. They think of prayer as something they are "supposed" to do. They tell themselves, "Others around me are always praying. And the pastor is always provoking us to pray. Besides that, the Bible calls for prayer. So, I have to pray. It's just the Christian thing to do."

Others pray only when tragedy strikes or when a crisis befalls them. And they do not pray again until the next difficulty comes along.

Beloved, the church will never understand the importance of prayer until we grasp this foundational truth:

> PRAYER IS NOT JUST FOR OUR OWN WELFARE OR RELIEF—BUT FOR THE DELIGHT OF THE LORD!

Unless these two elements go together, we do not have a foundation upon which to build a prayer life. Prayer is not just for our benefit—but for the delight of our God! We are not just to intercede for things we need, but to ask for the things He desires.

Christians can be very self-centered and selfish when it comes to prayer. Often we go to the Lord only to unburden our troubles and sorrows to Him—to seek a supply of strength for the next battle. Of course, that is Scriptural; we are invited to come boldly to God's throne of grace, to find mercy and help in our times of need. He has told us to cast all our cares upon Him.

But our praying is not complete—it is not prayer that is most pleasing to the Lord—if we do not understand God's need! Whereas we seek relief and help from the Lord, He desires fellowship with us—intimacy and communion.

Our primary purpose in praying ought always to be fellowship with the Lord. After all, He already has made every provision for our daily needs:

"...Take no thought for your life, what ye shall eat, or what ye shall drink; nor yet for your body, what ye shall put on.... Behold the fowls of the air...your heavenly Father feedeth them. Are ye not much better than they?

"...your heavenly Father knoweth that ye have need of all these things. But seek ye first the kingdom of God, and his righteousness; and all these things shall be added unto you. Take no thought for the morrow..." (Matthew 6:25-26, 32-34). "...for your Father knoweth what things ye have need of, before ye ask him" (verse 8)."

God is saying to us: "When you come into My presence, focus your attention on fellowship with Me—on getting to know Me. Don't let your focus be on material things. I know what your needs are. You don't even have to ask—I'll take care of them all! Just seek Me. Let us enjoy sweet communion!"

Yet, how much of our prayer time is spent asking God for a better job, a better home, food, clothes and other necessities? If most Christians subtracted such petitions from their prayer time, there would be little or no prayer left!

Perhaps prayer is a burden to you. Do you pray mostly out of a sense of obligation? Is prayer boring to you? Is it more of a duty than a pleasure?

So few Christians enter God's presence with delight, simply for the pleasure of His company. Some think of it only as "work"—labor, exertion, effort. Yet, when we commune with a dearly loved one here on earth, do we think of it as work? No—that is a pleasure to us! If you are happily married, you don't think of your times of intimacy with your spouse as "work."

How many marriages have been ruined by a mate who thought of intimacy only as duty? There is a generation of older Christian women who taught their daughters that intimacy with a husband was only a difficult, burdensome duty. They considered it to be work, an obligation, with no delight at all.

Yet Christ likens His relationship with His people to that of a husband and wife—and the Bible says Jesus delights in us! The fact is, a husband's pleasure in enjoying intimacy is not simply the satisfaction of his own needs. No—his real pleasure is in the joy of knowing his wife shares his delight. He says in his heart, "She really wants to be with me. I'm first in her heart—I'm everything to her!"

She is not reluctant to enjoy intimacy with him. She doesn't see it as a duty or obligation. Rather, she delights in him. And when he reaches out to her, she reciprocates by reaching out to him. They delight equally in each other.

We know the Lord delights in His people. The Bible tells us: "How fair and how pleasant art thou, O love, for delights!" (Song of Solomon 7:6).

And David said, "...he delivered me, because he delighteth in me" (Psalm 18:19).

Can you imagine the Lord being exuberant with delight over His children? That is the picture Scripture gives us. Our God delights in us!

Yet, do we delight in Him? The Bible tells us the Lord should be our delight:

"Delight thyself also in the Lord; and he shall give thee the desires of thine heart" (Psalm 37:4).

"...I sat down under his shadow with great delight, and his fruit was sweet to my taste" (Song of Solomon 2:3).

Now, delighting in the Lord doesn't mean simply being gleeful or happy in His presence. I asked the Lord what the expression "delighting" means. He answered:

"David, delighting in Me means simply being able to say: 'I would rather be with Jesus than with anyone else on earth! I prefer His company even over that of my spouse, my family, my friends. I prefer Him over all celebrities, world leaders, famous people, even great men and women of God. I would rather spend time with Him than with anybody else. He is my delight!'

"It also means being able to say, 'I long to be shut in with Him—because He is the only One who can satisfy me. All others leave me empty and unfulfilled. No one but Jesus can touch my deepest needs. And I rush to Him as often as I can!'"

Indeed, Jesus is waiting for us with every resource—everything we need for comfort, strength and power. Yet, often we either sit and brood in His presence, or we rush off to phone a friend to try to find help. Can you imagine what that must do to His heart?

Our "delighting" is something the Lord recognizes in us. He knows when we are drawn to His presence. If we truly delight in Him, everything that hinders us from coming to Him will bother us. We'll grow lonely, heartsick for Him, knowing that nothing else can touch or fill that deep spot in our hearts. No prayer can be wholly pleasing to Him until He is assured we come to Him because we prefer Him. He wants to know that above all else!

> COMING TO THE LORD WITH DELIGHT DOES NOT MEAN WE CANNOT COME TO HIM WITH SADNESS AND GRIEF.

Keep in mind my definition of "delighting in the Lord"—that is, preferring to be with Him above all others. This gives new meaning to our times of being sad, downcast, heavy-hearted, confused. To whom do we run in such times? Whose company do we prefer then?

Hannah is an example of a woman who came daily into the Lord's presence. She came to the temple sad of heart—weeping, with a sorrowful spirit. "And she was in bitterness of soul, and prayed unto the Lord, and wept sore" (1 Samuel 1:10).

Hannah shared her husband with another wife, Peninnah, who had borne several children. Hannah had remained barren, and Peninnah harassed her about it day and night. Scripture says this woman "provoked (Hannah) sore" (verse 6), making her life miserable.

Now, Hannah was dearly loved by her husband. But even he could not comfort her nor abate her sorrow. He said to her, "...am I not better to thee than ten sons?" (verse 8). Yet Hannah must have thought, "You don't understand. I have a need you can't meet!"

So Hannah stood before the altar weeping, sorrowful, with a deep groaning in her spirit. She testified to Eli, the priest: "...I am a woman of a sorrowful spirit: I...have poured out my soul before the Lord....out of the abundance of my complaint and grief have I spoken hitherto" (verses 15-16).

Hannah was not afraid to come into the Lord's presence with her sadness. In fact, in her sorrow she preferred His company. Yet many believers today simply will not come into God's presence because they are sad, downcast, weeping, broken, going through trials. They say, in essence, "I don't want to offend God by coming to Him this way. I'll wait till I'm happy and joyful before I come into His presence."

We're accustomed to going before the Lord corporately with hand-clapping, praises, joyful worship. But this account of Hannah makes it clear we're to come to Him even in our saddest moments. And, as Hannah was in intimate prayer with the Lord, He spoke peace to her heart: "...So (she) went her way, and did eat, and her countenance was no more sad" (verse 18).

This passage tells me: "Don't hide from the Lord. Don't run anywhere else. Run straight into His presence, and weep it all out before Him! Tell Him everything you're going through. Let Him have all your sadness."

Yet we all tend to shy away from the Lord during our sad times. I recently had a time of unexplained sadness. There was no real reason for it; it was just one of those heavy times I couldn't understand. I hesitated to go to prayer that morning, thinking, "I'll wait till this evening. Then I'll be okay. I can have my time with the Lord then."

But the Holy Spirit prompted me to turn to the book of Nehemiah. As I read chapter 2, I saw something I hadn't seen before. This chapter contains an encouraging story for all who come to the Lord with a heavy heart.

Nehemiah was a cupbearer to King Artaxerxes. He tasted the wines before they were brought to the king's table, making sure they weren't poisoned. Over time, Nehemiah became a trusted servant to the king.

Now, Nehemiah had received a report from his brother Hanani that Jerusalem was in ruins. The population had been decimated, the people were in terrible straits, and conditions were worsening daily. This tore at Nehemiah's heart. He loved Judah and Jerusalem—and a sorrow and sadness began to grip him. Scripture says:

"And it came to pass...I took up the wine, and gave it unto the king. Now I had not been beforetime sad in his presence. Wherefore the king said unto me, Why is thy countenance sad, seeing thou art not sick? this is nothing else but sorrow of heart. Then I was very sore afraid..." (Nehemiah 2:1-2).

You must understand—people were forbidden to come into the king's presence with sadness, especially if they were court employees. Nehemiah knew this could have cost him his head, and he was terribly fearful.

But the king was moved with compassion when he saw the grief of Nehemiah. Scripture tells us he gave his downcast servant a leave of absence. He also gave him a letter of credit, opening the royal treasury to him. Nehemiah then received from the king the desire of his heart—permission to go to Jerusalem to rebuild the temple and city walls!

Here is my point: If it were possible for Nehemiah to go into the presence of a pagan king with a sad, heavy countenance, and yet find favor, compassion and blessings beyond imagination—how much more will King Jesus show compassion to each of us His children in our sadness, lifting our burden and supplying our need? Would a pagan king show more mercy to a downcast servant than our all-merciful Savior and King would?

Perhaps at this point you are confident you love the Lord and delight in Him. You have learned to run to Him just for the pleasure of His company. And in your wonderful times of intimacy with Him, He lifts all your burdens and floods your soul with peace, joy, assurance of His love.

But is that the end-purpose of prayer? Is it to give us ecstasy—to provide us with rest and peace? No! There is much more to this matter of praying in a way that's pleasing to God:

> IF WE ARE GOING TO PRAY IN A MANNER PLEASING TO THE LORD, WE MUST LEARN TO PRAY THROUGH!

"Praying through" is a term coined by the early Pentecostals. To some it meant simply staying on your knees until you were assured you had an answer from God. To others it meant continually coming back to the Lord until you had the answer in hand. (This was also called "persevering in prayer.")

As a young boy in those early camp meetings, I heard people testify, "I'm going to lay hold of the horns of the altar—and I won't let go until God answers!" Yet I don't believe that is the truest meaning of "praying through."

You can be shut in with the Lord on the Mount of Transfiguration, delighting in His presence. You can spend quality hours, even days, with Him, glorying in sweet communion. You can have all your needs met. Your heart can be totally satisfied. His presence can heal you, lift you, empower you, strengthen you.

But what happens when you leave that hallowed place of intimate communion? You may rise up from your knees only to go back to a crushing situation that has not changed. You can see the devil waiting there for you, ready to throw the same problems and emptiness at you. I ask you: What good is it to get the glory on the mountain if it won't see you through your battle?

Let me explain what I believe is meant by "praying through." The phrase means simply this: The strength, power and encouragement you receive from the Lord while shut in with Him must see you through the trials ahead! The victory you get in the secret closet has to give you victory on the battlefield.

Think about it: What exactly did you get from your time of prayer, if it wasn't something that could see you through the battle? Was yours a "completed" prayer? You see, "praying through" means waiting for the completion of your prayer—that is, for total completion. Many Christians see only half-answered prayers—because they don't allow what they received from the Lord in prayer to carry them through their trial. Indeed, many sincere prayers have been wasted, aborted, lost—because they were not "carried through" in this way.

How many of us have gone to the Lord in prayer, unburdening our hearts to Him—and afterward were lifted out of a pit, our joy restored, our faith rising up? The first thing He tells us in our time with Him is, "Don't be afraid. I am with you." He settles our spirit, bringing us rest and peace. And we go out of His presence feeling strong, ready to fight the good fight.

But what happens the next day, when a trial arises? How do you react when your circumstances begin to fall in on you? Do you collapse after only a short while?

Many of us get discouraged when our circumstances don't change after much prayer. We believe God for a change—and, indeed, many times He does bring one about. But in the times when He doesn't, we often go from a wonderful mountaintop experience straight into a battle—and we fail miserably!

Beloved, prayer is not finished—it is not "completed prayer"—until it sees you through to the other side of your trial. We have not "prayed it through" until we have "lived it through"—that is, lived through our trials by the strength we received in God's presence.

God fully intends that what He gives us in prayer will fully supply us with everything we need for our battle. He wants to give us something powerful enough to see us through any situation—to place us above the battle!

I must confess, this is where I fail most in prayer. I have known and enjoyed the ecstasy of intimacy with my Lord; He has become my delight. I know what it is like to run to Him with heaviness, sorrow, tears flowing—and to experience His awesome touch, filling me with peace and relief. But when I face the next trial or crisis that comes along, all of my peace and joy seem to evaporate. I discover I have not yet prayed through!

Has this ever happened to you? Perhaps you went to church and were blessed, coming out of the sanctuary with a sense of power and anointing. Yet, when you got home, you got into an argument with your spouse. Then you went to work on Monday, and everything went wrong. Where, at that moment, was the joy, peace and rest you got from being in the Lord's presence not long before? Your prayer has not been prayed through!

Somewhere between the glory and the crisis, we lose everything we gained during our intimacy with the Lord. So, how can we keep it? What can we do to see our prayer through to a triumphant conclusion?

I have prayed about this continually because of the many Christians everywhere who are hurting so badly. Our ministry receives between 30,000 and 40,000 letters a month from our readers—and I have never heard of such pain as I now read in these letters.

Many Christians are suffocating from a loneliness that is so bad, they can hardly see themselves through a day. Others are suffering through all kinds of marital and family problems. Pastors are grief-stricken over all the hurting people in their congregations.

As I read of such grief, I have to cry out to God, "Father, I can't write a message that will add to their burden. Please, Lord—what am I to say?"

The answer I received is the message I am writing to you today: The Lord wants you to receive something from your intimate time with Him—to have a power and authority that will carry you through your trials. He wants you to pray through them completely!

"But how?" you ask. "How can I maintain the victory I receive in my prayer time with Him? How can I take it through to the other side of the battle?"

There are two things we must do to pray through our trial:

THE FIRST WAY WE LEARN TO PRAY THROUGH IS BY LISTENING!

Most Christians don't listen to God. They go to Him only to talk! Yet the Scriptures reveal that any person who was ever used of God learned to remain in His presence until hearing from Him.

Scripture makes it clear the Lord wants to talk to every one of us: "And thine ears shall hear a word behind thee, saying, This is the way, walk ye in it, when ye turn to the right hand, and when ye turn to the left" (Isaiah 30:21).

I heard of a little girl who was dying of leukemia. As she neared death's door, she struggled with the thought of dying. Yet one morning, when her mother came into her room, the girl was all aglow and happy. "What has happened to you?" her mother asked.

The little girl answered, "An angel came to me and said I was going on a trip. God came and took my hand and walked with me through a beautiful garden. He told me, 'You're coming here tomorrow, to be with Me.'"

God spoke to that little child—and took all the pain and fear from her heart! When she left to be with Him the next day, she had total peace.

Tell me—when you are intimate with Jesus, do you receive such direction from Him? Does He tell you what to do—and when and how to do it? Some Christians don't believe God does this. But Jesus says, "My sheep hear my voice...and they follow me" (John 10:27).

There is no way through your trial, except to get alone with Jesus and cry, "Lord, You're the only One on this earth who can help me. Only You know the way through this trial. So I'm going to stay

This is the kind of "praying through" that is pleasing to God! It means stopping everything, all activity, until you hear His voice. Only then will you hear Him speak clearly to your heart: "You've got to make things right with this person..." Or, "You've got to make restitution here..." Or, "Just stand still till next week. Don't get in a hurry. Sit in My presence and trust Me..." He will give you clear directions!

Yet, something even more is needed for us to see our prayers through the coming trials—to make our prayers complete:

THE SECOND THING NEEDED TO PRAY THROUGH IS TO ADD TO OUR INTIMACY TOTAL CONFIDENCE IN GOD'S WORD!

Christ is the living Word of God. And when you are shut in with Him in prayer, the Holy Spirit will always lead you to God's revealed Word. He will build up your faith by feeding you from the Bible—even while you're in the secret closet! We are commanded:

"Put on the whole armour of God, that ye may be able to stand against the wiles of the devil.... Wherefore take unto you the whole armour of God, that ye may be able to stand in the evil day... And take...the sword of the Spirit, which is the word of God" (Ephesians 6:11, 13, 17).

Often when you receive specific instructions from the Lord, His Spirit will whisper, "Now turn to...", directing you to a passage of Scripture. God's Word will speak to you directly—telling you how to get through your crisis!

Right now, there are many Christians reading this message who simply have to hear a word from the Lord. Nobody on earth can help them. There is but one way for them to get through their trial—and that is by staying in Christ's presence until He gives them direction! He must tell them the way through—what to do, and when and how to act. His exclusive direction to them won't come one minute too early or too late. It will all be in the Holy Ghost's timing!

Dear saint, there is no need for you to worry about your trial. God is faithful to respond to your every need and request. So, as you go to prayer now, simply pray, "Lord, I come now not just to have my needs met—needs You have foreseen and are eager to supply. No—I come also to meet Your need!"

God, put in all of us a heart that is easily wooed to Your presence. Help us to pray through all our trials to completion...to listen closely to Your Spirit in our secret time of communion with You...and to put all our confidence in Your revealed Word. In these ways, we can know our prayers are pleasing to You. Amen!

—David Wilkerson was the founding pastor of Times Square Church in New York City. There he ministered to gang members and drug addicts. In 1971, he founded World Challenge, Inc., which supports missionaries and outreaches throughout the world. He died in 2011.

Reprinted by permission: World Challenge, Inc., PO Box 260, Lindale, TX 75771.
http://worldchallenge.org.

HOW TO FOLLOW GOD'S VOICE - IN INTERCESSION

LESSON 4

THE HOLY SPIRIT AND INTERCESSION

MAIN PRINCIPLE

God is eager to give the Holy Spirit to those who ask. The Holy Spirit prays with us and for us according to God's will. God still seeks those who will specially give themselves to prayer guided by the Holy Spirit.

HOW TO FOLLOW GOD'S VOICE - IN INTERCESSION

THE LISTENING SIDE OF PRAYER

by Stacey Padrick

HOW TO HEAR GOD'S VOICE ABOVE THE CLAMOR

God desires for us to be intimate with Him. If we are going to go deeper in our walk with Him, then we need to develop that intimacy. And true intimacy with God requires more than just speaking to Him—it involves listening to Him as well.

I used to think, *If only God would speak more clearly, I would follow Him more closely.* I have often complained that His still small voice seemed too still and too small. But at unexpected times, when I became quiet for a few moments—stopping from my jog to watch a sunset, or gazing at a starry evening sky while taking out my trash—I have heard Him, the voice of a friend, a friend longing to be heard and waiting for my ears to be open and attentive.

God desires to communicate with His people, even more than we desire to communicate with Him! He is still the same God and continues to speak to us, if only we have ears to hear. I have learned to hear His voice through listening prayer—what some call contemplative prayer.

Contemplative prayer isn't simply prayer for those who are more reflective in personality. It is for introverts and extroverts alike. You may think of contemplative prayer as a practice only of saints and mystics in by-gone eras. But it is not limited to a particular type of person, a particular era, nor is it reserved for the "super spiritual"—those who seem to have an intimacy with God we have not experienced.

Contemplative prayer is a form of prayer that all believers today can enjoy.

WHAT IS CONTEMPLATIVE PRAYER?

So what exactly is contemplative prayer? How can we in our world of incessant noise and activity incorporate it into our daily lives? Contemplative prayer is thoughtful, reflective prayer. It requires effort. Rather than a passive form of prayer, it demands active listening, focused attention, and confident expectation that God will speak.

In contemplative prayer, we are still before God, reflecting, anticipating, listening, and waiting on Him. Throughout the Psalms, David models one who waits on God in this way: "My soul waits in silence for God only" (Ps. 62:1, *NASB*). "My soul thirsts for God, for the living God. When can I go and meet with God?" (Ps. 42:2).

Contemplative prayer is *being* with God, empty-handed, waiting attentively for whatever He wants to speak, to show, or to do. It is the discipline of being still, knowing that He is God (Ps. 46:10).

If contemplative prayer is not an elaborate form of prayer reserved for monks, why don't we practice it? We discipline ourselves to meet regularly with God for supplication, intercession, and Bible study. Why is simply sitting at His feet with no agenda so difficult—even frightening?

Most of us argue that we haven't "enough time." Those of us who have taken time may complain that God doesn't seem to speak clearly. But upon closer inspection of these excuses in my life, I recognize other reasons for my avoidance. I am afraid of what I might

Discipleship Journal

hear. When I quietly wait on God, the Holy Spirit often speaks penetrating words—words of conviction, words of love, or no words at all.

With *words of conviction*, God reveals actions or attitudes I need to confess to Him and sometimes others and directs me to seek reconciliation.

On many occasions, as I take time to listen to God, the Holy Spirit reminds me of a recent conversation and a comment I made that was neither edifying nor necessary. Had I not taken time to allow His Spirit to bring this to light, I would not have recognized the hurt I caused Him and another person. Only by listening to the Spirit's conviction can I recognize my sin and hear Him direct me to seek forgiveness from my friend.

At other times as I listen, God has exposed attitudes of mine that dishonor Him. For instance, when I have been wrought with anxiety about a situation I face, He has revealed that my anxiety reflects a lack of trust in Him—in both His concern for me and His ability to work in and through my crisis.

> WHY IS SIMPLY SITTING AT HIS FEET WITH NO AGENDA SO DIFFICULT—EVEN FRIGHTENING?

Surprisingly, I often find myself just as reluctant to hear His *words of love*—particularly when offered apart from anything I have done or plan to do for Him. When I anxiously strive to please God by my works yet fall short of my expectations, I feel less than lovable. Hearing then His words of grace and love can be painfully difficult. Like an uncomely peasant girl who withdraws in shame at the beckoning words of love from a handsome prince, we too are sometimes afraid to hear the powerful whispers of love from our great Prince. His amazing love shines light on our darkness and gently calls us out of hiding and pretense to be with Him.

Many of us don't wait in His presence long enough to let Him love us. We are quick to voice our concerns, seek His guidance, and request His blessing. Yet, how it must grieve our Father's heart that we come to Him only in want of something, rather than coming simply because we enjoy being in the Father's presence.

Perhaps another reason we hesitate to practice contemplative, listening prayer is we fear hearing *no words at all*. Influenced by our product-oriented culture, we strive to attain some tangible result validating the use of our time, even our devotional time with God. So afraid of "wasting time," we become unable to enjoy the delight of simply being with Him. Yet, as two lovers are content to be in each other's presence, not needing always to speak, God delights for us to sit at His feet and enjoy being with Him.

PUTTING IT INTO PRACTICE

How can we begin to practice contemplative prayer? The following are suggestions to explore. They are not meant to be formulas. Ask God to show you additional ways to incorporate contemplative prayer into your life.

1. **Meditate on Scripture.** "I will meditate on your precepts" (Ps. 119:78).

   After studying Scripture, choose one verse, phrase, or word upon which to meditate. Ponder it. Slowly repeat it. Ask the Lord what He wants to speak to you through it. Perhaps check the dictionary to attain the full definition of a word.

   For example, choose a verse such as, "The Lord is my shepherd, I shall not be in want" (Ps. 23:1). Sometimes, such a familiar verse loses its meaning. Meditating upon it and asking questions reveals what we may be overlooking: What is a shepherd's role and responsibility toward his sheep? Are sheep able to help themselves? Do I have want? Have I asked God to provide for me in that area? What is He saying to me about my needs?

   Take time to savor each word, that you may taste the riches of His spiritual food and its nourishment for your life.

2. **Sing and pray the Psalms.** "Sing praise to the Lord" (Ps.68: 32).

   After reading a psalm, begin to sing it to a tune you know or create as you go along. I find that singing a psalm helps me ponder it afresh by increasing my involvement in what I am reading. Try praying the psalm as if you had written the words from your heart.

   Or learn from those who for centuries have chanted the Psalms. During my stay at a monastery, I joined the monks as they chanted a few chapters of the Psalms each morning and evening.

3. **Journal in prayer.** Write your prayers to God and wait for His response. Writing helps us stay focused and enables us to probe our thoughts and heart more deeply.

   Try a new exercise called "Dialogue with God." Write something you want to tell God (for instance, a statement—rather than a question—about something happening in your life). Then listen for His still, small voice. Asking the Holy Spirit to guide you, write what you sense is His response to your statement. Continue the dialogue until you believe God has finished speaking to you.

For example, while struggling with a chronic illness, I wrote in my journal: *Stacy: O Lord, I know You can heal me. God: Yes, I can heal you, but I want to heal your spirit first. Will you let Me heal your spirit and wait on My timing to heal your body?*

When I first learned this exercise, I was very reluctant. How presumptuous to think I could write God's response to me! Yet, I beheld with amazement His words to me through this exercise—words very different from what I expected to hear. He has often brought Scripture to mind or emphasized that which I already know but am having difficulty believing. Through this exercise, God also points out the enemy's lies I have been listening to and directs me to claim His words of truth. I recommend writing with a Bible nearby to refer to as He leads.

4. **Take a walk in nature and listen to God speak to you through His creation.**

"The heavens declare the glory of God; the skies proclaim the work of his hands. Day after day they pour forth speech; night after night they display knowledge" (Ps. 19:1-2).

When I take time to thoughtfully observe God's creation, He tangibly teaches me His Word. While I sit alone on a beach, absorbed in the power and constancy of the waves, He reminds me that His love for me is consistent: "The LORD'S loving-kindnesses indeed never cease, for His compassions never fail. They are new every morning" (Lam. 3:22-23 NASB). Running my fingers through the sand around me, I remember David's words, "How precious to me are your thoughts, O God! How vast is the sum of them! Were I to count them, they would outnumber the grains of sand" (Ps. 139:17-18). Looking out toward the vast ocean, I ponder, "If I settle on the far side of the sea, even there your hand will guide me" (Ps. 139:9-10).

5. **Be still before Him.** "The LORD is good to those who wait for Him, to the person who seeks Him. It is good that he waits silently . . . Let him sit alone and be silent" (Lam. 3:25-26, 28, NASB).

°In this posture of stillness, we can more keenly hear Him speak. We honor God by expressing our willingness to be still in His presence.

We may find it difficult and uncomfortable at first to relinquish our needs-oriented approach to prayer. But I firmly believe we delight God's heart when we come to Him not to receive or give Him anything, but rather simply to delight ourselves in Him (Ps. 37:4). Do not ask for anything. Instead, allow Him to express His love and joy over you.

If total stillness is difficult, try the following exercises. After closing your eyes and stilling your body, become aware of your breathing. As you slowly inhale, think on a name of Jesus:

- Meditate on this name as you slowly speak it to yourself, reflecting upon all that it means; for example: Bread of Life, Good Shepherd, Master, Light of the World, the Vine, the Door, the Resurrection and the Life, Alpha and Omega.
- Or meditate on the name of God: Deliverer, Rock, Strong Tower, Jehovah-Jireh (Provider), Jehovah-Rapha (the Lord who Heals), I AM, Abba.
- A similar exercise helps when I am anxious. I slowly inhale, saying to myself Jesus' name, and with each exhalation I release a fear or worry that is on my mind. Then, I continue to think on Jesus' name, yet each time I exhale I think on a characteristic of Jesus; for example: my hope, my joy, my peace, or my righteousness. There is power in Jesus' name.

Try scheduling a longer period of time once a week for contemplation. Reflect on the events of the week, conversations, unexpected news, a sermon, or something you are reading. I like to see it as "making a date with God." In our fast-paced world, many of us realize we have to make dates even with spouses or others close to us so we can have quality, one-on-one time together. Why not make a date with God, apart from your devotional, as time to "hang out" with Him? Go for a walk alone with Him, or sit with a cup of coffee and talk to Him freely, listen, and enjoy being with Him.

Developing a discipline takes perseverance. Our flesh does not like to be trained and controlled. We will find every reason not to practice contemplative prayer: Things must be done, phone calls must be made, worries crowd our thoughts. As we sit in silence, we will itch and squirm, our backs will ache, and our stomachs will grumble. But as we sit with Him in faith and obedience, He will honor our desire to know and hear Him. Do not be discouraged if you do not hear anything. God often wants us to sit in stillness at His feet and learn to be content in His presence. Pray for

Discipleship Journal

the desire and grace to communicate with God in this intimate way.

—Stacey S. Padrick is a freelance writer, speaker, and part-time real estate investment manager. She is author of *Living with Mystery: Finding God in the Midst of Unanswered Questions* (Bethany House).

Copied from the DISCIPLESHIP JOURNAL: 1996 © by The Navigators. Used by permission of NavPress. All rights reserved.

HOW TO FOLLOW GOD'S VOICE - IN INTERCESSION

FLAKY INTERCESSION

Flak´y (fla´ke), adj. Exhibiting eccentric, unbalanced or irrational behavior.

By Cindy Jacobs

The phone rang early one Monday morning. The caller, a young Bible student, Pam (not her real name), had been attending a large church that emphasized prayer.

"Cindy," she said, "I don't want to be disobedient to God, but something is not right with my prayer group." As Pam told her story I realized she was involved with flaky intercessors.

How did it happen? One Sunday morning at church a woman I'll call "Estelle" approached Pam with a "word from God" that she was to join a select home prayer group and intercede for the pastor. Estelle shared excitedly that this group would be asked to become the pastor's personal intercessors and travel with him when he was on the road.

At that time, though, Estelle failed to tell Pam that neither the pastor nor the church leadership knew of this select group. Estelle, Pam later discovered, was expecting God to supernaturally reveal it to them.

> A GOOD PRAYER FOR INTERCESSORS IS "LORD, SHOW ME MY HEART SO I CAN REMAIN PURE BEFORE YOU ALWAYS."

Without checking to determine if the church's leaders were aware of and endorsed the prayer group, Pam decided to attend some of their meetings. At first they seemed to pray some "right on" prayers, but after a few meetings they began praying in a direction exactly opposite of the vision of the church.

They fervently prayed that the pastor would "see the light and get aligned with God"—which in their minds was synonymous with getting aligned with them. They also prayed that God would lead him to consult with them regarding direction for the church. This made Pam extremely uneasy and prompted her to call me.

I recommended that Pam leave Estelle's group and join the church-sponsored intercessory meeting for reasons that I will discuss later in the article.

BIRTHED IN PRAYER

Pam's situation is fairly typical of the problems that my husband, Mike, and I frequently hear as leaders of "Generals of Intercession," a Christian organization dedicated to bringing major ministries together to intercede for the nations. She was sucked into a group of "flaky intercessors," men and women who for a variety of reasons drift outside biblical guidelines in their zeal for prayer, thus bringing reproach on their ministries and confusion and division in the church.

Flaky intercession could become a widespread problem, for I believe—and many prophetic voices are proclaiming—that God is calling the church to intense prayer and intercession as a prelude to revival.

Studies of past revivals indicate that they were birthed and bathed in prayer. However, the inability to sustain effective intercession short-circuited the move of the Holy Spirit. In many instances, it was flaky intercession that undermined true prayer and destroyed revival.

In a recent planning meeting for a post-Lausanne II Consultation on Cosmic-Level Spiritual Warfare, I sensed the Lord speaking this word to me about an upcoming reformation in the church: "In the time of Luther, the rallying cry was, 'The just shall live by faith.' In the coming reformation, the watchword will be, 'We wrestle not against flesh and blood, and the weapons of our warfare are not carnal.'"

Satan, the crafty, evil serpent that he is, undermines revival through one of his most effective weapons—deception. Through clever lies that appeal to the flesh he draws people away from God's purposes for revival prayer. In other words, he works overtime at making flaky intercessors. So, how do we avoid flaky intercession?

The answer is actually quite simple. Use clear, biblical guidelines as your plumb line for intercession. In the remainder of this article I will introduce three guidelines that act as effective firewalls to flaky intercession.

ACCOUNTABILITY

First, intercessors need *spiritual accountability*. Go back and look at Pam's situation at the top of the article. Estelle's prayer group was flaky because they were lone rangers; they were off doing their own thing.

There was no submission to the church's leadership, and the direction and leadership of their group (including Estelle) had not been confirmed by the pastor.

This is not to say that it's wrong to have prayer groups in the home, but I always ask people if they have their pastor's blessing before starting one, and if they are committed to an on-going, submitted relationship to church leadership.

Spiritual accountability is comfort and protection since God intends that the prayer life of the body be life-giving to the church. If there is fear of having our prayers and revelations judged, then we are on flaky spiritual ground.

CLEAN HEART

A second guideline is what I call the *clean-heart principle*. Psalm 51:10 says, "Create in me a clean heart, O God." Estelle violated this principle in several areas. For one, she had pride in her heart. She was convinced that she needed to be a leader rather than submit to the leadership of prayer groups established by the church. She felt that her revelations were far superior to what the pastor or any of the elders heard from God. (This is a common trap for some people when God begins to share some of his secrets with them through prayer.)

Estelle had also developed a critical spirit, which is closely associated with the sin of pride. She was critical of the way intercessory groups had been set up by the pastor, especially since she had not been asked to lead one. Estelle did not know her own heart. She should have become involved with an established prayer group in the church, proven herself as trustworthy, and then let God promote her (or *not* promote her) to leadership.

As intercessors we need to ask God to reveal the heart motives behind our prayers. I have observed that many aspiring intercessors pray out of bitterness and wounded spirits. What I find remarkable is that they are unaware of their heart conditions. They are drawn to intercession because of its great power and, subconsciously, because they see it as a means of getting their way. This was the case for Estelle; she was unhappy about the direction of her church.

Only God's Spirit is capable of revealing the true condition of our hearts. Therefore a good prayer for intercessors is "Lord, show me my heart so I can remain pure before you always."

THE WORD

Another guideline for avoiding deception is to *pray the word*—seeking God's will for a given situation and then praying it back to him.

> STUDIES OF PAST REVIVALS INDICATE THAT THEY WERE BIRTHED AND BATHED IN PRAYER.

When I first learned to pray the word, I had a little book with topic headings and related Scriptures for almost any situation. If someone had a need, I just turned to the appropriate section of the book and prayed directly from it.

One day a woman I will call Beatrice phoned with a dire financial need. Would I pray? Boy, would I! I prayed every prosperity Scripture in my little book and any other passages I could think of. I also told the devil to get his hands off her finances. I felt quite satisfied with my spirituality.

On hanging up, however, I sensed that the Holy Spirit was grieved; so I prayed again, and God began showing me that he had been dealing with the woman about getting a job and that she was resisting him because of laziness. Her financial need had resulted from disobedience.

I realized that she was unrepentant, and I had prayed against the dealings of God in her life! I was shaken and quickly asked for God's forgiveness. Since then I have sought God for his *living* word for each situation in which I minster.

This is a critical point to grasp. *We must learn how to pray God's word.* Some people pray cafeteria-style; they go through the word of God searching for parts that fulfill their appetites—especially the blessings. "God," they pray, "I want a new house, the neighbor next door for my spouse…oh, and please throw in a new car for good measure, because your word says, 'Whatsoever things you desire, when you pray, believe that you have received them and you shall have them.'"

Well, God's word is full of promises and blessings, and in many specific instances he may want to give us a house, wife, or car. But assuming everything that he wants is God's will is not the same as praying *God's Word*. First, we must ask what he wants for us; then we are free to petition. Otherwise, prayer becomes presumption—which is flaky intercession.

Perhaps as you read this article you are sensing God's call to deeper intercession. If so, allow me to introduce you to the best safeguard from flaky intercession—the Holy Spirit. *He* doesn't want you to get into deception; he wants to come alongside and teach you how to pray. Here's a prayer to help you get going:

Father, I pray that you would send your Holy Spirit on me now and search my heart that I may be found pure and clean… Give me a heart for your word that I may intercede only according to your truth… Fill me now with your Spirit that I might know how to pray…Place a passion for intercession within me that I might share in the high calling of advancing your kingdom. Amen.

— Cindy Jacobs is a respected prophet who travels the world ministering not only to crowds of people, but also to heads of nations. Cindy has authored several books, including *Possessing the Gates of the Enemy, The Voice of God and The Power of Persistent Prayer.* Cindy loves to travel and speak, but one of her favorite pastimes is spending time with her husband Mike, two grown children and their adorable grandchildren.

Reprinted by permission: Equipping the Saints

LESSON 5

PERSEVERANCE AND HOLINESS

MAIN PRINCIPLE

We must walk in holiness before the Lord so that our prayers can be effective. Persistence and perseverance have an important role in our prayer life.

HOW TO FOLLOW GOD'S VOICE - IN INTERCESSION

WHO ARE YOU?

by Barbara Shull

In recent years both secular and Christian counselors have repeatedly encouraged people to find the answer to the question, "Who am I?" However, this idea of the importance of knowing who you really are is not new.

In a letter to first-century Christians the Holy Spirit inspired Paul to write, "Be honest in your estimate of yourselves" (Rom 12:3 TLB). This Scripture infers that you are not to think that you are better than you really are, nor worse. Paul admonished the reader to know the truth, to face the honest facts.

Why is knowing your true identity necessary to an intercessor? Because honesty is the basic foundation upon which any relationship and communication is built. When you received Jesus into your life, you were born a second time, this time of the Holy Spirit. In other words, you became a child of God directly related to Him (John 1:12-13).

Inherent in this relationship is the need and/or desire to communicate with your heavenly Father and He with you. Prayer is one avenue through which you communicate your desires to God. There are many avenues through which He communicates His love to you.

Think about your earthly relationships. If you pretend to be someone you are not when around a particular person, your communication with that person will only reach a certain level. As you lay aside your masks and have an honest, open, transparent relationship with each other, your communication can be more productive and worthwhile. You can enjoy this deep kind of communication with God and, in fact, become increasingly effective at it, as you get to know and accept the real facts about God and the real facts about yourself.

The first truth you need to know and accept about yourself is that you are naturally sinful, proud, selfish, and unholy. Within every single one of us is a rebellious nature that wants to do its own thing, go its own way, and build its own kingdom (Isa. 53:6). Paul expressed this truth when he said, "For I know that nothing good dwells in me, that is, in my flesh" (Rom. 7:18 NSB). The Living Bible paraphrases this verse, "I know I am rotten through and through so far as my old sinful nature is concerned."

If you are ignorant of this fact, you may be shocked and distressed when the Holy Spirit convicts you of sin. The temptation at that point is to condemn yourself for not doing as well as you thought you ought to have done. Either that or you will rationalize the ungodly characteristics you see in your life by blaming others. "If my husband didn't buy those goodies, then I wouldn't overeat the way I do" ... "I wouldn't get uptight if she would do her job" ... "If only the children would behave, then I wouldn't lose my temper."

If you don't blame other people, you may blame the devil. Yet, if our ungodly behavior is caused by our sinful nature rather than by Satan, we are "beating the air" (1 Cor. 9:26 NASB) and will wear ourselves out battling the wrong adversary.

The balancing factor, the other side of the fact that you are a sinner, is the liberating truth of who you are in Christ. The moment that you, by faith, accept Jesus and what he has done for you personally by the shedding of His blood, two life-changing aspects of His grace take effect.

First, He justifies you. To be justified is to be "just-as-if-I'd" *never sinned*. What a miracle! To those who are sinful and unholy, He gives His garment of holiness. To those who are unrighteous, he gives the free gift of His righteousness (2 Cor. 5:21, Gal. 2:16). You are then in right relationship with God; you have immediate access into God's holy presence (Col. 1:20-22), where you have the privilege to worship, petition,

April 1998, Charisma

and intercede, being free from all condemnation.

Secondly, when you accept Jesus as Lord and Savior, God's Holy Spirit comes to live in you. He furnishes you with the power to change, little by little, into His very own likeness (2 Cor. 3:18). So begins the purifying process of being made righteous and holy in experience. The gift of righteousness given at the time of rebirth is instantaneous; being made righteous is a gradual lifetime process. Both are characteristics of the born-again child of God.

In order to enjoy honest, open fellowship and communication with God, you need to keep both these truths in balance: who you are *without* Christ, and who you are in Christ.

However, if you focus on only one truth or the other, you will become unbalanced. If you emphasize on the righteousness God has graciously given to you, overlooking the fact that you as a redeemed sinner need to constantly repent and change, you are not being honest with God or with yourself. It is possible to ignore a particular sin, quote a Scripture about the righteousness you now have in Jesus, and presume that you can still come boldly before God. While virtually nothing can separate you from the love God has for and demonstrates to you in Jesus (Rom. 8:38-39), you know yourself there are times when you have sinned and need to get right with God. You may feel a separation until you confess and repent of your sin. As you do, the Lord's merciful forgiveness and cleansing of your repentant heart will restore your fellowship and communion with Him.

While you need to face your sins honestly, it is extremely dangerous to concentrate on your sinful nature. Unhealthy introspection is likely to produce self-pity and depression among other things, which will deaden your sensitivity to God and hinder your praying.

You can avoid either extreme if you ask God to reveal who you really are, encompassing both sides of the truth. Spiritually free Christians can say, "I am an unholy sinner, but I am robed in Jesus' righteousness and am being transformed into His image, actually being made holy."

As you know and are honest about who you are, you will be more secure in your relationship with the Lord and can then focus your attention on Him, instead of yourself, and go about the daily business of living.

You may be sure that there will be times when He exposes a new part of your basic, prideful nature, a specific weakness, a sin, or wrong motive. As you face this exposure, confess your sin, and ask for the forgiveness that is yours because of the blood shed of Jesus. Then, by faith, you can receive the grace to repent and change, and continue your walk with God.

The skill of knowing and being honest about who you really are so that you can enjoy a close and constant relationship with God is an absolute necessity for an intercessor.

— Excerpted from Barbara Shull's book, *How to Become a Skilled Intercessor* published by Women's Aglow Fellowship, Lynwood WA (now Aglow International, Edmonds WA).

Reprinted with permission from Women's Aglow Fellowship

April 1998, Charisma

HOW TO FOLLOW GOD'S VOICE - IN INTERCESSION

CONSECRATION: A PARTNERSHIP WITH GOD

by Kent Henry

We have entered into a partnership with our heavenly Father concerning holiness by making our lives available to be His holy vessels. In many ways we have fallen down on our end of the agreement by not walking in a higher level of moral excellence, some of us through ignorance and some of us through disobedience. But the end result is the same. This is the hour to begin to change.

Living A Separated Life

"Consecration." I keep hearing this over and over in my spirit. This is the season to purify our lives and begin to live a truly God-filled, separated life. It is no small undertaking considering the amount of ungodly "trailings" that have been left in our lives from the world and religious indoctrination. Yet, we can cleanse ourselves, not by might, nor by power, but by the Sprit of God.

Consecration has two basic elements that demand our attention and understanding. One, God has consecrated us to the work of His service in the earth by the blood, death and resurrection of Jesus Christ our Savior and Redeemer. Two, there is our daily responsibility of walking out our consecration in obedience to the Word of God.

The embodiment of three of the primary Hebrew words for consecration gives us an example we can use as a model. "Qadash", (Kaw-dash') means "to be clean ceremonially or morally;" "nazar" (naw-zar') is defined as "abstaining from impurity, to set apart;" and "charam" (khaw-ram') is to seclude, specifically to devote to religious use."

Made To Be Clean

"Qadash" meant that God could make, pronounce or observe to be clean, either ceremonially or morally. In Christ, we have received this standing. Our heavenly Father has made us clean through the blood of Jesus. II Cor. 5:21 states it clearly: "He made Him who knew no sin on our behalf, that we might become the righteousness of God in Him (Jesus Christ)." We were declared ceremonially, even morally, clean.

In Exodus 28:41 it says, "And you (Moses) shall put them (priestly garments) on Aaron your brother and on his sons with him; and you shall anoint them and ordain them and consecrate them (dedicate, hallow, purify, sanctify [wholly]), that they may serve as priests."

A similar calling has been given to each member of the Body of Christ, to serve this generation as consecrated priests to and before the Lord. Rev. 1:6 says that "Jesus made us kings and priests (literally a kingdom of priests), unto God." A real revelation of this fact does yield a higher motivation for living a life worthy of a son of God, a member of the Body of Christ, a joint-heir in the royal priesthood.

Called to be Priests

A major missing element in the church today is that the call to be priests has gone forth, but very few are living the lives essential to priesthood. Many Christians are now living on the extreme outer edges of the Biblical standards for upright living.

God's idea of purity and holiness is much higher than the currently accepted standards of most Christian circles. Corporately, in the body of Christ, we haven't had an overwhelming number of brilliant, shining examples to model our lives after or an overabundance of concentrated Biblical teaching affirming these areas of personal consecration. But this cannot be an on-going excuse to keep us from changing, nor used as the only reason why others have fallen far short of God's standards in the past.

April 1998, Charisma

Abstain from Impurity

The second Hebrew word, "nazar," tells us about another necessary part of consecration, which is, "to remain aloof or abstain from impurity." Numbers 6 spells out the law of the Nazirites. These men took a vow before the Lord to live a life of abstinence from certain things. In this case, as it is recounted, the unshaven hair was to be an offering to the Lord.

The point for us today is not to become legalistic in our approach to abstinence, but rather to follow after the principles put forth in the Bible. We must also follow through in obedience when the Holy Spirit directs light on an area of our lives, exposing the error of our way.

Many of us hear the "word of the Lord," but don't follow through and change our lives in order to become consistent to that Word. It is not necessarily an issue of heart as much as an issue of permanence. It's not good enough to obey for only a few days, or weeks or months. We have to tear down and remove "all the high places" on a permanent basis.

A Secluded Life of Devotion

Finally, the word "charam" completes the consecration picture. We can remove ourselves and abstain from impure things, but we must also reciprocate by "secluding" ourselves away and "devoting" ourselves to God. There is a mental and spiritual attitude that over-takes a person as he spends consistent, quality time in prayer. It's the mindset that he, as a priest of the Lord, has a special, covenant relationship to keep himself unstained from the weight of ungodly things. It is done in the same spirit as a woman keeping herself for her husband. It is a very holy thing to the Lord.

To the Hebrew people, living a separated life was a primary object in their lives. To most of us who were brought up in a Gentile nation, our personal standards are usually left to our own imaginations. The Hebrew people would have been reviled if they practiced some of the attitudes and lifestyles that were so readily accepted, even blatantly followed, in their day. It should suffice to say that we, as believers, in trying to walk in a scriptural and godly fashion, must guard against being drawn into and persuaded to follow worldly ways. It may not be popular, but it is God's priestly way. In Leviticus 27, there are three verses (21, 28 and 29) that sum up the heart of things devoted to the Lord. Verse 28 declares, "Anything which a man sets apart (devotes or consecrates) to the Lord out of all he has . . . shall not be sold or redeemed. Anything devoted (consecrated) to destruction is most holy to the Lord." A man in those times knew what it meant to devote something to the Lord. It was something costly. Living a secluded life before the Lord is costly as well. It involves your whole life. Unless you lose it, you can't gain the higher things of God in their deeper measure.

— Kent currently is live streaming worship and the Word five days per week across multiple online platforms from the Carriage House Ministries studios in St. Louis, MO.

Reprinted with permission: Psalmist Magazine

April 1998, Charisma

HOW TO FOLLOW GOD'S VOICE - IN INTERCESSION

FINDING GOD IN YOUR WILDERNESS

by Alice Smith

During football season, once again we find Lucy holding the football for Charlie Brown to kick. But just as his foot is about to make contact, she moves the ball, sending him sprawling to the ground. Aggravated yet still trusting, he tries again and again. Each time he goes flying. Finally in frustration he turns and asks, "Where do you go to give up?"

No doubt each of us has looked for the "giving-up place" at some juncture of our Christian walk. For me it has most often happened when I've found myself in a spiritual "wilderness."

When the Heavens Are Brass

Spiritually speaking, what is the wilderness—and how do we know we are there? The silence of God and the absence of His felt presence is one of the ways we recognize the wilderness. Other evidences include:
- The heavens are brass. Our prayers seem to reach only the ceiling.
- Intimacy is gone. There is a sense of barrenness in prayer.
- We suffer feelings of spiritual rejection, loneliness and abandonment by God. We have no meaningful encounters with Him in prayer.

The spiritual wilderness can come in many ways. It can come through *external circumstances* that cause significant changes in our lives—a job loss, a move to a new location, family difficulties or relational struggles. It can also come through *traumatic events* like the death of a friend or loved one; divorce (the death of a marriage); the missing of a life goal or the fading of a dream; or sin—whether our own or one committed against us.

One of the more difficult wilderness times my husband, Eddie, and I experienced occurred in 1993. We had been nestled in a comfortable place in the ministry for more then 11 years, and we had no interest in moving.

But the Lord had something else in mind.

Our intercessors began sharing with us their impressions that we were in a stage of transition. Our ministry as we knew it was about to be restructured, they said. Although we valued the insights of the intercessors, it was my hope that they were totally wrong on this one.

However, by late summer it was obvious that the time had come to change directions. The Father moved us into a corner where we were forced to either go forward or disobey.

Without any further instruction, direction or plans for long-term income, we resigned from the church we had started almost 12 years earlier. Leaving a church we planted, trying to explain to loved ones why we had done so and still trusting the Lord for our future was painfully difficult. It was similar to a death.

The grief in the days that followed was overwhelming. We had no understanding. My solace was found only in the prayer closet, but even then I would sit numbly before the Lord.

The heavens were closed to me. Questions flooding through my mind while I cried to the Lord for help. The enemy accused me of missing God.

Two months later, still stuck in the wilderness, I felt led to start a 40-day fast. The first 30 days in prayer were heavenly as I experienced a glorious recovery of my usual intimacy with Jesus. Then it ended. Physical fatigue set in.

April 1998, Charisma

> WHETHER YOU LIKE IT OR NOT, GOD WILL SEND YOU TO THE WILDERNESS AT SOME POINT IN YOUR LIFE. DON'T RESIST—LET HIM LEAD YOU THROUGH THE DRY PLACES AND INTO A DEEPER RELATIONSHIP WITH HIM.

The last 10 days were a battle I will never forget. The assault from the enemy was unrelenting.

Deadness settled over me like a blanket. I began to understand in a minute way the spiritual warfare Jesus must have known the last three days before His crucifixion.

On day 30 of my fast, C. Peter Wagner from Fuller Theological Seminary called Eddie. "I believe the Lord is saying you are the man to start the United States 'prayer track' for the A.D. 2000 & Beyond Movement," he said. "Will you do it?"

What I didn't know was that Peter had called Eddie one month earlier with the same offer, and Eddie had declined. This time he agreed to at least talk and pray with me about it.

Immediately, I knew this was the direction for us.

Within weeks the Lord provided the new U.S. Prayer Track with an office, computer, a fax machine and volunteers. Hope, direction and revelation were renewed—and our wilderness faded away.

Our Response in the Valley

Perhaps you, too, have had times when you found yourself in a place of loneliness or darkness, overwhelmed by a sense of the silence of God. You are not alone! Some people refer to this wilderness as "the valley" or "the dark night of the soul."

The fact is, the Christian life is not lived in a constant "springtime" of new life and fast growth. There are seasons in our walk with the Lord. From time to time we will each experience the cold blast of a spiritual "winter."

Such times can prompt a variety of responses, some productive, some counterproductive. For example:

- *Questioning.* We may ask such things as, "What are You doing, Lord?" Or "God, where are You?" Or negative suggestions such as the following may enter our minds: "The Lord must not love me, because He is letting the devil do this."

In the wilderness, the devil attacks us with lies about the Father. He presents us with options other than trusting the Lord with our lives. He tries to force us to sin or to get ahead of God's plan.

Early on we need to make a choice to trust God and not the devil so that we don't falter in the midst of testing.

- *Apathy.* Someone once said, "When God puts you on hold, don't hang up." If we are not careful, the wilderness can produce discouragement, and discouragement can result in apathy. Like Charlie Brown, we may begin to look for a place to give up.
- *Introspection and faultfinding.* Although it is good to allow the Lord to examine our hearts and reveal any hidden sins, too often we adopt a "woe is me" mind-set. We begin to analyze ourselves, our situations and others. In so doing, we become critical and can eventually suffer "analysis paralysis."

Responses like these are just what the enemy wants. He wants us to question God's commitment to us and our commitment to God. Satan wants us to be critical and negative. When he engages us in spiritual battle, he wants to see us wave the "white flag."

Don't entertain the enemy! If you give him a toehold, he will take a foothold. And if you give him a foothold, he will build a stronghold.

The Purpose of the Wilderness

The wilderness is necessary. Yet we tend to misunderstand our need for the wilderness experience because we have not learned the ways of God.

> "THE CHRISTIAN LIFE IS NOT LIVED IN A CONSTANT 'SPRINGTIME' OF NEW LIFE AND FAST GROWTH."

King David said, "He made known His ways to Moses, His acts to the children of Israel" (Ps. 103:7, NKJV). Most of us are seeking God's *acts* when we should be learning His ways. It is through His *ways* that we will know Him. In our struggle for the anointing, a manifestation or power in ministry, the Father often allows us to grope in disillusionment until we are willing to be Spirit-led, not need-driven.

April 1998, Charisma

The wilderness is necessary because it brings us to a place of brokenness. We may try to avoid it, but the reality is that brokenness is our friend, not our enemy. A quick look at Scripture shows this is true.

Jesus said, "Blessed are the poor in spirit" (Matt. 5:3). Isaiah tells us that God dwells "with him who has a contrite and humble spirit, to revive the spirit of the humble, and to revive the heart of the contrite ones" (Is. 57:15-16).

We often treat brokenness as if it is to be a one-time experience. It's not. As the late evangelist Mickey Bonner wrote, "Brokenness is the forgotten factor of prayer." Regardless of the circumstances that bring on our wilderness, the crucial issue is that we learn what the Lord is trying to teach us.

Certainly, one of those lessons is to trust in Him. Too often, we assume the silence of God is a sign of His rejection of us. Not true! He has promised never to leave us or forsake us. But He has also promised to grow us up in Christ.

It is easy to overlook the reality that it is in the valley where things grow. On the mountaintop there is hard rock and exposure to the elements. But down below, in the valley, there is nutrient-rich soil that produces a bountiful harvest.

The psalmist declared that *God enlarged* him when he was "in distress"—that is, in the valley (see Ps. 4:1 KJV). We need to trust that He will do the same for us.

I believe there are many other reasons the heavenly Father allows the silence to come into our lives. Perhaps the most important is to keep us constantly in pursuit of Him. Too often we take for granted the privilege of experiencing His presence and hearing His voice. Our God is a jealous God—jealous for our time and devotion.

Furthermore, He wants us to learn to depend on Him, not on ourselves. His desire is for us to stay calm and unperplexed in the midst of turmoil. We glorify the Father when we accept the process of internal brokenness rather than striving for an end.

We should not forget that it is our God who prepares a table before us *in the presence of our enemies* (see Ps. 23:5). The person who has no trials has no triumphs! Yet we tend to want the victories without the battles that, by definition, must precede them.

Learning in the Wilderness

Jesus explains in John 12:24-25: "I tell you the truth, unless a kernel of wheat falls to the ground and dies, it remains only a single seed. But if it dies, it produces many seeds. The man who loves his life will lose it, while the man who hates his life in this world will keep it for eternal life" (NIV). I call this one of the Bible's "upside-down principles"—a way of thinking that is opposite to the way the world thinks.

Jesus teaches if you want to *live*, then you must *die* (see Phil. 1:21). If you want to receive, then you must give (see Luke 6:38). For Christ to *increase*, you must *decrease* (John 3:30). To be *exalted*, you must *humble* yourself (Matt. 23:12).

> "THE WILDERNESS IS A NECESSARY ENCOUNTER. IN IT, A DEEPER INTIMACY AND DEPENDENCY UPON GOD IS FORGED."

Wilderness experiences may seem like frozen, dead times. But God teaches us a great deal in them if we are willing to learn. For example, the wilderness:

1. **Crucifies false spirituality.**

   In the wilderness, we begin to take off our phony "spiritual masks" that have been hiding our true love of self. Our carnal, soulish nature believes that self-effort, plans, projects, and spiritual disciplines will prove our worth before God and others. However, in the valley the Lord strips away false piety and foolish expectations about our own abilities and success.

2. **Reinforces God-dependence**.

   We can never endure the wilderness without a profound sense of the Father's unconditional love and acceptance. The wilderness times do not come so He can torment us or because He is angry with us. They are opportunities to build a deeper faith and stronger determination to follow Christ.

   The danger of falling along the way is real. The Israelites were challenged with several wilderness trails—and many fell. Numbers 14:32 states, "But as for you, your carcasses shall fall in this wilderness" (NKJV).

   We must not resist the breaking that comes through suffering. We must take the bitter with the sweet and let the bitter make us better. We must understand the Father is more concerned about our holiness than He is about our happiness.

3. **Prepares us for new levels of revelation.**

   In life, the wilderness always precedes revelation. Christ could not be glorified until He had first

April 1998, Charisma

been crucified, nor can we. Don't forget Jesus was led by the Spirit into the wilderness temptation (see Luke 4:1-2).

But He emerged from the wilderness in the power of the Spirit (see Luke 4:14). Jesus set the example for us all by walking through the wilderness, accepting the experience with faith in God and coming out of His testing with a greater anointing.

Jesus' experience shows us a cycle Christians go through: wilderness, then revelation, then victory, then blessing. If we do not struggle against the process, the result can be amazing breakthrough and unprecedented communion with the Lord.

The wilderness experience is ultimately a paradox and a mystery of our faith. We will never be able to understand the mind of God; His ways are higher than our ways.

But know this: The wilderness is a necessary encounter. In it, all confidence and pretense of the flesh is washed away, and a deeper intimacy and dependency upon God is forged.

For Charlie Brown, the frustration of circumstances led to a desire to give up and throw in the towel. But for those of us who go through the wilderness and learn its lessons, we have strength and hope to go on—no matter what comes our way.

— Alice Smith served as Prayer Coordinator for the U.S. Prayer Track of the A.D. 2000 and Beyond Movement. Former pators, Alice and her husband Eddie, are cofounders of the U.S Prayer Center in Houston, Texas.

Reprinted by permission Charisma Magazine and Strang Communications Company

April 1998, Charisma

HOW TO FOLLOW GOD'S VOICE - IN INTERCESSION

LESSON 6

INTERCESSION FOR THE FAMILY

MAIN PRINCIPLE

We have the honor and responsibility of praying for our families. As we intercede on behalf of our family, we need to ask God what His hopes and plans are for them, and pray accordingly.

HOW TO FOLLOW GOD'S VOICE - IN INTERCESSION

INTERCESSION

by Kent Henry

With all the talk of prayer and spending time with God, I am concerned that believers may grow accustomed to the message, and fall short of doing it.

As I travel from place to place, it seems as if many Christians still have not chosen the lifestyle of prayer. Christians are called to live a life of closeness, even nearness to the Lord.

Prayer, praise and worship are powerful vehicles for many things. A lifestyle of praise and prayer keeps us flowing in the fruits and gifts of the Holy Spirit. A lifestyle of closeness to God is surely a safety net that keeps us from the ravages of sin. A believer who praises, worships and prays a lot is a person guaranteeing themselves fulfillment of their potential and destiny.

Living to Make Intercession

One of our jobs is to be like Jesus. Scripture says of Him: "He ever liveth to make intercession" (Heb. 7:25). As believers, we can get into the harness and help pull against the things that are hindering God's people and His kingdom. One way to effectively fight the enemy is through intercession. We learn how to pull down the strongholds of the enemy and understand our God-given authority against the wiles of Satan.

II Cor. 10:3-5 says, *"For though we walk in the flesh, we do not war according to the flesh, for the weapons of our warfare are not of the flesh, but divinely powerful for the destruction of fortresses. We are destroying speculations and every lofty thing raised up against the knowledge of God, and we are taking every thought captive to the obedience of Christ."* To do this takes a commitment to seek God's heart and to pray for those to whom He directs us.

Individually, we should all be intercessors to some extent. As priests of our homes, we husbands need to intercede for our families. I pray for length of days and fullness of time for my wife and kids regularly, for protection from any accident that would befall them or me. I never let my children go anywhere without praying over them. This is a lifelong commitment until they fulfill God's calling on their lives. Set a time and begin interceding for your family.

In a similar way, we should be praying specifically for individuals, such as pastors or missionaries, or for the Christians behind the Iron Curtain. Intercede for others on a consistent basis. In 1 Timothy 2:2, we are instructed to intercede for "all those in authority." We need to set aside a time on a weekly basis to hold up our church elders, worship leader and pastor. As we pray for them, our prayers release God to minister to their needs.

Fill in the Gap

One of the gravest verses in the Bible is Ezekiel 22:30, where it says the Lord sought for a man to "make up the hedge and stand in the gap before Him" but He found no one.

The church has always seemed to lack a multitude of strong intercessors. Yet every one of us should be willing to stand in the gap for the lost, and intercede for the redeemed. But it takes discipline and the "every-day-ness" of prayer to do it. God looks for people with His heart; people who will carry His burdens for His purposes in the earth.

One group of people that the Lord has put on my heart are those with "shipwrecked faith." They are the ones who were young in the Lord, or ungrounded in spiritual things who watched some strong Christians, someone they trusted deeply, fall from righteousness. Those young believers got shook up so badly that they lost their faith and fell away. They quit serving the Lord because they didn't know what else to do.

If we prayed half of these people back in to worshipping, solid churches, the results would greatly benefit God's kingdom. I pray for them to return; to be grounded and strengthened in the faith once more.

There will be a special group of people for which you will feel led to intercede. Let the Lord speak to your heart about them. Follow the impulses of the Holy Spirit.

Lift Up the Afflicted

One of the highest callings is to lift up the afflicted. 1 John 3:15 says, "Hereby we perceive the love of God, because He laid down His life for us: and we ought to lay down our lives for the brethren." We can bless the unrighteous and the godly by praying for them. One way to love your enemies is by lifting up their needs for salvation and knowledge; a way to love the Body of Christ is to pray consistently.

One other point is this: your work is not finished once you get off your knees. Intercessors are doers. After Esther fasted and prayed, she went in to the king and persuaded him to change the law of the land. Ezra cried out to God in prayer and afterward, went to work with Nehemiah rebuilding the wall. How do you think God is going to lift up the afflicted in your city or any place else without using you?

God has chosen each of us as an instrument of His righteousness on earth. He has made us His hands and feet to those people who need help.

The burden doesn't stop with prayer. It always evolves into action. I say, "put feet" to your praying. Once you've prayed, then obey the promptings of His Spirit.

— Kent currently is live streaming worship and the Word five days per week across multiple online platforms from the Carriage House Ministries studios in St. Louis, MO.

Reprinted with permission: Psalmist Magazine

HOW TO FOLLOW GOD'S VOICE - IN INTERCESSION

COURAGE IN THE INNER COURT

by Derek Prince

Though today's news is dominated by the actions of presidents, kings and governments, it is my conviction that our world is ruled by those people *who know how to pray.*

Looking back through history, I see the ministry of intercession as God's method of answering problems that cannot be resolved in any other way. Thus intercession is truly one of the highest ministries open to any Christian.

Some intercessors work quietly behind the scenes, yet exercise with power the gift God has given them. Then there are those who are called to openly intercede—or stand in the gap—for people or causes. Moses, for example, was constantly standing between God and His chosen people, pleading for them. Abraham did this for Sodom and Gomorrah. Such intercessors are especially close to the heart of God.

Queen Esther was one of these intercessors. Her Old Testament story has much to teach us about the faith that is needed for this kind of intercession. Esther was a lovely Jewish maiden in the Persian Empire at the time of the exile of her people from Israel. She was an orphan who had been brought up by her uncle, Mordecai, an important official in the court of the Persian emperor.

Because she was not only beautiful in looks, but also in spirit, Esther had been chosen to be queen of the Persian Empire, a position of tremendous influence and importance in the emperor's palace. However, at Mordecai's insistence, Esther had never publicly revealed the fact that she was Jewish.

After she became queen, a certain anti-Semite official named Haman tricked the emperor into signing a decree that would put to death all the Jews in Persia on the false grounds that they were disobeying all the emperor's laws. The plan, if carried out, would result in total destruction of the entire Jewish nation.

When this decree went forth, Mordecai sent a message to Esther in the queen's palace that it was her responsibility to persuade the king to change his mind about the decree.

Esther's reply: "For any man or woman who approaches the king in the inner court without being summoned, the king has but one law: that he be put to death. The only exception to this is for the king to extend the gold scepter to him and spare his life. But thirty days have passed since I was called to go to the king."

Mordecai sent back this answer: "Do not think that because you are in the king's house, you alone of all the Jews will escape. For if you remain silent at this time, relief and deliverance for the Jews will arise from another place, but you and your father's family will perish. And who knows but that you have come to royal position for such a time as this?"

Then Esther sent this reply to Mordecai: "Go, gather together for prayer all the Jews who are in Susa. Also have them fast for me. Do not eat or drink for three days, night or day. I and my maids will fast as you do. When this is done, I will go to the king, even though it is against the law. And if I perish, I perish."

So Mordecai went away and carried out all of Esther's instructions (Esth. 4:11-17, NIV).

What a picture of an intercessor. Note the commitment!—"If I perish, I perish." Whether Esther lived or died was not the most important question, but what she could do for her people.

Esther also knew that there are times when praying, alone, is not enough, thus she asked her people to fast three days and three nights.

Imagine her tension when she went to the palace three days later and stood in the inner court, facing the king's hall. How would he respond? Was she going to her death?

April 1986, Charisma

When the king saw Esther, he was pleased with her and held out to her the gold scepter that was in his hand. Then he asked her, "What is your request, Queen Esther? Even up to half the kingdom, it will be given you."

At this point victory was won for the Jewish people. It is always won, I believe, through intercession. When Esther then boldly revealed to the king Haman's plot to destroy her people, Haman was put to death and his palace given to Queen Esther.

Note this beautiful fact about Esther. When she went to the king, she didn't go as a beggar and she didn't grovel. She put on her royal robes. She stood there in his presence, a lovely queen. She took her rightful position.

I believe the same applies to you and me as Christians. We're to recognize who we are in God's sight—the position that God has elevated us to. We are not to grovel. We are not to go as beggars. In one sense, these words from the 52nd chapter of Isaiah describe Esther: "Awake, awake, O Zion, clothe yourself with strength. Put on your garments of splendor, O Jerusalem, the holy city. The uncircumcised and defiled will not enter you again. Shake off your dust; rise up, sit enthroned, O Jerusalem. Free yourself from the chains on your neck, O captive Daughter of Zion" (v. 1-2).

Those men and women who have mastered the art of intercession have the following:

1. Intimacy with God.
2. Boldness in approaching God.
3. Conviction of God's absolute justice, both positive and negative, that God will spare the righteous but judge the wicked.
4. A concern for God's glory and, conversely, a disregard of personal interest and ambition.
5. A dedication to the task, even at the cost of life itself.
6. Willingness to identify with those for whom we intercede.

— Derek Prince was a prolific Bible teacher and author, who devoted his life to the teaching and study of the Bible and became internationally recognized as a leading authority on Bible prophecy. His legacy continues through Derek Prince Ministries, dedicated to the proclamation of the Gospel around the world.

Reprinted by permission Charisma Magazine and Strang Communications Company.

April 1986, Charisma

SCRIPTURES FOR PRAYING FOR THE FAMILY

Read the following verses and make prayers out of them for your loved ones.

For unsaved family members:

Psalm 146:8—That the Holy Spirit would open their eyes to see who Jesus is and that God would lift them up.

Isaiah 42:16—That God would draw them to Himself.

1 Timothy 1:13—That the Lord would show them mercy.

Psalm 68:18—That God would lead them out of bondage.

Proverbs 21:1—That God would direct their hearts.

Proverbs 1:10, 15—That they would seek the right kind of friends and be protected from the wrong kind.

Hosea 2:6-7—That they would not find their way to wrong people or places and wrong people would not find their way to your loved ones.

For saved family members:

Philippians 1:6—That God would complete the good work He began in them.

Hebrews 12:2—That Jesus would perfect their faith.

Colossians 2:2—That God would encourage their hearts, unite them with other believers in love, and give them complete knowledge of Christ.

Ephesians 1:17-19—For wisdom and revelation, and for knowledge of the hope to which God has called them and His great power for them.

Ephesians 3:16-19—For strength in their inner beings, faith in the indwelling Christ, experience of God's immeasurable love for them, and complete filling by God.

Proverbs 1:10, 15—That they would seek the right kind of friends and be protected from the wrong kind.

Psalm 97:10—That they would hate evil.

1 Corinthians 6:18-20—That they would be kept from impurity.

Galatians 5:22-23—That the Holy Spirit would bear His fruit in their lives.

Galatians 5:16—That they would walk by the Spirit and not gratify the desires of their flesh.

Romans 12:1-2—That they would be totally devoted to Jesus.

LESSON 7

PRAYING FOR PEOPLE GROUPS

It is on the heart of God that His people pray for the Holy Spirit to snatch many people groups around the world from the judgment awaiting them. He desires that all would come to a saving faith in His Son Jesus. Though God can do whatever He wishes, He has chosen to use us as His vessels for His glory.

HOW TO FOLLOW GOD'S VOICE - IN INTERCESSION

HOW TO PRAY FOR THE LOST

by Dutch Sheets

IN RESPONSE TO OUR PRAYERS, GOD CAN REMOVE THE BLINDNESS THAT PREVENTS UNBELIEVERS FROM SEEING THEIR NEED FOR THE SAVIOR.

I watched the cesarean section delivery of a baby on television once. I had always figured the doctors just cut the woman's skin and out plopped the baby. No way! They pert-near (that's Texan for "nearly") turned that poor lady inside out. They pulled out and pointed out things I didn't even know were there.

When they finally got to the baby, it was all they could do to tug him out. I don't know why he held on like he did. If he had been able to see what I was seeing, he would have wanted out fast.

Believe it or not, that program helped me understand an important aspect about spiritual warfare for the lost—about interceding for those who don't know Christ. The Bible says there is a veil that keeps unbelievers from clearly seeing the gospel. "If our gospel is veiled, it is veiled to those who are perishing, whose minds the god of this age has blinded, who do not believe, lest the light of the gospel of the glory of Christ, who is the image of God, should shine on them" (2 Cor. 4:3-4, NKJV).

The word "veil" means "to hide, cover up, wrap around." The Greek word is *kalupsis*. The inside of a human body is veiled by skin, for example.

The New Testament word for revelation is simply *kalupsis* with the prefix *apo* added—*apokalupsis*. Apo means "off or away," so literally a revelation is an unveiling, an uncovering. As I watched that surgery, I understood a little better about the nature of a "veil."

Letting in the Light

It is important to know that unbelievers don't see the gospel because they *can't see it*. They don't understand it because *they can't understand it*. They must have an unveiling—a revelation.

It used to be difficult for me to understand how some people could hear and reject powerful gospel presentations. Now I know. They didn't hear what I heard, see what I saw or understand what I understood. What the unbelievers heard was filtered through a belief system—a veil—that caused them to hear something totally different.

The distorted perception the unbeliever has is illustrated by the story of the woman who was driving home alone one evening when she noticed a man in a truck following her. Growing increasingly fearful, she exited the freeway and drove up a main street, but the truck stayed with her, even running red lights to do so.

In a panic, the woman wheeled into a service station, jumped from her car and ran inside screaming. The truck driver ran to her car, jerked the back door open and pulled from the floor behind her seat a man who was hiding there.

The lady was fleeing from the wrong person. *She was running from her savior!* The truck driver, perched high enough to see into her back seat, had spied the would-be rapist and was pursuing her to save her, even at his own peril.

Likewise, people run from a God who desires to save them from destruction.

Those of us who know Him realize we love God because He first loved us. When sinners, however, hear of a loving God who wants only their best and

July 1997 Charisma

who died to provide it, they often see instead only the promise of loss and a lack of fulfillment.

Unbelievers need to "see the light." The word "light" in 2 Corinthians 4:4 is *photismos,* which means "illumination." Our English word "photograph" is derived from this Greek word.

What happens when one takes a photo? The shutter on the camera opens, letting in light, which projects an image. If the shutter on the camera does not open, there will be no image and thus no picture, regardless of how beautiful the scenery or how elaborate the setting.

The same is true in the souls of human beings. It makes no difference how glorious our Jesus is or how wonderful our message; if the veil (shutter) is not removed, there will be no true image (picture) of Christ.

Oh, sometimes we talk people into a salvation prayer without a true revelation, but there is usually no real change. That is why fewer then 10 percent—I've heard figures as low as 3 percent—of people who "get saved" in America become true followers of Christ.

There is no true biblical repentance, which comes only from biblical revelation. Jesus told Paul he was calling him "to open their eyes"—to bring enlightenment, unveiling, revelation, repentance—"in order to turn them from darkness to light" (Acts 26:18, italics added).

> "THE UNBELIEVER CAN'T WAR FOR HIMSELF. WE MUST TAKE UP OUR DIVINE WEAPONS AND FIGHT IN PRAYER

Information vs. Revelation

We need to understand—and I'm afraid most do not—the difference between *information* and *revelation*. Information is of the mind; biblical revelation, however, involves and affects the mind, but originates from the heart.

Spiritual power is released only through revelation knowledge. The written word *(graphe)* must become the living word *(logos)*. This is why even believers must do more than just read; they must also abide in or meditate on the Word, praying as the psalmist did: "Open my eyes, that I may see wondrous things from Your law" (Ps. 119:18). The word "open" here *(galah)* also means "unveil or uncover."

Information can come immediately, but revelation is normally a process. As the parable of the sower demonstrates, all biblical truth comes in seed form.

God once told me: "Son, all truth comes to you in seed form. It may be fruit in the person sharing it, but it is seed to you. Whether or not it bears fruit depends on what you do with it." Seeds of spiritual information must grow into fruit-producing revelation.

Why is this so important? Because without revelation the fallen, selfish, humanistic mind is always asking, *What's in it for me?*

When we appeal to this mentality through human wisdom and intellect alone, we often preach a humanistic, what's-in-it-for-them gospel, and we produce—at best—humanistic, self-centered converts.

If, on the other hand, we preach a pure gospel, including repentance and the laying down of a person's own life (acknowledging the lordship of Christ), unbelievers are sure to reject it unless they receive a biblical revelation: "But the natural man does not receive the things of the Spirit of God, for they are foolishness to him; nor can he know them, because they are spiritually discerned" (1 Cor. 2:14).

We must allow the Holy Spirit time to birth true repentance in them through God-given revelation. This produces God-centered Christians, not self-centered ones. God knows we could use some of those, especially in America.

God's Holy Detonators

How does Satan blind the mind of the unbeliever? What gives place to this veil?

The word "blinded" in 2 Corinthians 4:4 (KJV) is *tuphloo*, which means "to dull the intellect; to make blind." The root word, *tupho,* has the meaning of making smoke, and the blindness referred to in this passage is like a smoke screen that clouds or darkens the air in such a way as to prohibit a person from seeing.

From this same root comes a word *(tuphoo)* that means to be high-minded, proud or inflated with self-conceit. When I saw the connection between the words *tuphloo* and *tuphoo* and their definitions (blindness and pride), a major missing link was supplied for me.

When we approach people on a human basis, especially if they think we are pressuring them, we generally make things worse. This is because the root of pride in them that says, *I don't want anyone else controlling me or telling me what to do*, rises up and defends itself. If we attack this pride on a human level, we will only strengthen it.

July 1997 Charisma

On the other hand, we have weapons that are "divinely powerful" to pull down strongholds if we would only realize it (see 2 Cor. 10:4-5, NASB). God says, "Instead of using your weapons, I'll let you use Mine. Yours won't work; Mine will."

The word "powerful" *(dunatos)* is actually one of the New Testament words for a miracle. These weapons empowered by God will work miracles.

The word is also translated "possible." I like that. Do you know anyone that seems impossible? Will it take a miracle? With this power, they become possible. And, of course, this is the Greek word from which we get the word dynamite. This stuff is explosive!

I remember watching, as a small child, the destruction of an old, brick school. I was fascinated as the huge cement ball, attached to a gigantic crane, was swung time after time into the building, crashing through walls and ceilings, bringing incredible destruction.

I suppose this would be in one sense a valid picture of our warfare as we systematically—one divine blow at a time—work destruction on the strongholds of darkness. We generally wage a systematic, ongoing, one-blow-at-a-time war against Satan's strongholds.

Yet, I saw another huge building in Dallas demolished several years ago. This edifice was much larger than the school I had seen destroyed as a child. It covered nearly an entire block. The demolition crew didn't use a wrecking ball. And it didn't take days—it took seconds. They used dynamite, strategically placed by experts to demolish the major structure in less than 10 seconds.

I like to think that this picture of rapid decimation can also be a reflection of the effects of our intercession. Unlike the destroyers of the physical building, we usually don't see the answer in seconds; we may be strategically placing the dynamite of the Spirit for days, weeks or months.

But every time we take up our spiritual weapons and use them against the strongholds of the enemy, we are placing our explosive charges in strategic places. And sooner or later the Holy Detonator of heaven is going to say, *Enough!* Then there will be a mighty explosion in the spirit, a stronghold will crumble to the ground, and a person will fall to his knees.

This Means War

Marlena O'Hern, of Maple Valley, Washington, had been praying for her brother, Kevin, to be saved for approximately 12 years with seemingly no result. "Kevin was heading down a rocky road. He had major problems, including drugs, depression and extreme anger," Marlena relates.

Early in 1995 she took a class in which I taught these principles about praying for the lost. Marlena and her family began to pray the principles over Kevin. They specifically prayed:

- That God would lift the veil off him (give him revelation)
- For the Holy Spirit to hover over him and protect him
- For godly people to be in his pathway each day
- That God would cast down anything in him that was exalting itself against the knowledge of God, specifically pride and rebellion
- To take down all known strongholds—thought patterns and opinions on religion, materialism and fear
- To bind Satan from taking Kevin captive and to bind all wicked thoughts and lies Satan would try to place in his mind
- That the armor of God would be placed on him.

After they had prayed for two weeks in this way, Kevin overdosed on drugs and in his time of need cried out to God.

"The Lord met him in a powerful way," Marlena says. "The veil was definitely lifted, and he had a revelation of God. He now has an understanding of the Word and responds to it. His focus is on pleasing God and knowing Him more and more."

First John 5:19 says, "We know that we are of God, and the whole world lies under the sway of the evil one" (NKJV). Yet we have been given authority! We can turn unbelievers "from darkness to light and from the power of Satan to God" (Acts 26:18). We are called to enforce and make effectual the freedom Christ procured.

The unbeliever cannot war for himself. He cannot overcome the darkness and understand the gospel until the veil lifts. We must take our divinely dynamic weapons and fight.

—Dutch Sheets is an author, teacher, pastor and speaker. Seeing America experience a sweeping revival and return to its godly heritage is Dutch's greatest passion. Some of his books include *Intercessory Prayer, The Pleasure of His Company* and *The Power of Hope.*

Reprinted by permission Charisma Magazine and Strang Communications Company

July 1997 Charisma

HOW TO FOLLOW GOD'S VOICE - IN INTERCESSION

PRAY UNTIL SOMETHING HAPPENS

by Doug Stringer

PRAYER IS SO MUCH MORE THAN HANDING A LIST OF REQUESTS TO GOD. IF YOU WANT EARTH-SHAKING RESULTS, YOU WILL BE REQUIRED TO TRAVAIL UNTIL HEAVEN'S PLAN BECOMES A REALITY ON EARTH.

God doesn't answer prayer. He answers desperate prayer." I can still remember my feelings of shock and bewilderment as Leonard Ravenhill, the late church statesman, spoke these difficult words to me.

Of course God answers prayer, I thought. But after much reflection I've come to recognize what Ravenhill meant: Often we approach prayer with the wrong attitude.

If we're honest with ourselves, we must admit that our prayers frequently degenerate into little more than religious incantations and shallow platitudes spoken out of a sense of religious duty. Yet the Bible compares prayer with the travail of childbirth.

It is, in essence, a passionate activity. I have found that it is often in times of desperation that I pray with a genuine passion to the Lord—a passion that allows no room for mediocrity or compromise.

That's the kind of prayer that God answers.

In November 1996 God led me to organize a time of passionate, city-wide prayer that became known as the Houston Prayer Mountain. For 40 days and nights, Christians gathered together across racial and denominational lines to pray, worship, repent and cry out for people to come to Christ.

One night, as men's ministry leader Ed Cole spoke to the group, he pointed to one of the banners on the platform. It read "P.U.S.H."—the acronym for "Pray Until Something Happens." That banner reminded him, he said, of a woman in labor being coached to "push, push, push" during the final stages of delivery.

His comparison rang true to us. We sensed that we were in a critical stage, pressing heaven for the birth of God's purpose for our city. In fact, the fourth chapter of Micah— which talks about a woman in labor and points to the process of "birthing" revival—was one of our themes.

Birthing Revival

Revival is coming—and it will arrive in one of two ways. It's interesting to note that the first part of Micah 4 is virtually identical to the first part of Isaiah 2, although the two chapters end differently. Micah 4 is a picture of revival by birth, while Isaiah 2 shows revival by judgment.

I believe it is God's desire to bring revival by birth—by our choosing it and pressing in for it—rather than by judgment—by His strong hand bringing us to our knees. Yet at times it may take a shaking to bring us to a place of genuine passion and intimacy with Him.

God's mercy is present even in His judgments. Better to be judged now than for eternity! For too long the church has tried to compensate on the outside—through programs, formulas and various styles of "window dressing"—for prayerlessness and a lack of truly changed character on the inside.

But what the Lord wants to do among us in our day is neither fleeting nor shallow; in the words of the children's song we sang during the Prayer Mountain, it is "deep and wide." For a move of God to be

March 1999 Charisma

deep and wide, there must be a revival of prayer and of godly character among believers.

The Lord's desire is that we bear fruit and fulfill His destiny for our lives. This is possible only if we become desperate enough to stop covering up our fears, pains, insecurities and sin and allow Him to replace our compensatory facades with His healing virtue and power.

God wants to take off our "cosmetic Christianity," our proverbial fig leaves. The first cover-up was not Watergate, Whitewater or Lewinskygate; it was "Figgate," as recorded in Genesis 3. We have been covering up ever since!

Instead of running to the Lord, our tendency is to cover up and hide from God. But God wants to change all that. He wants to satisfy the deep longing in our souls—in our spiritual wombs, if you will. He wants us to push.

Prayer Brings Intensity

More than 10 years ago, the Lord gave me a prophetic word that seems more appropriate now than when I received it in 1987. He showed me that we were being shaken by church and political scandals and by a constantly eroding foundation of morality and religious freedom.

I was reminded of Hebrews 12:25-29, which talks about a shaking so intense that only those things that cannot be shaken—those things built solidly upon the foundation of Christ's character and Word—would be left standing. The purpose of this shaking is to purify and mold us, and to cause us to see things from God's eternal perspective. God so desires that no one perish that He goes to great lengths to get our attention.

The Lord showed me that three things will take place through this shaking:
- He will bring His sheep and shepherds into line—except for those who reject His final call. The shepherds who have been off track will be shaken and brought back through the Lord's stern, merciful and loving hand.
- Any "mountains" standing in the way of the gospel will be moved aside if they do not repent. Any "fig trees" that are only cosmetic—that fail to produce true fruit—will be removed unless they become productive again.
- The rain of the Holy Spirit will fall on those who, while perhaps feeling forsaken and weary in well-doing, nevertheless persevere through God's refining. Those who have sought to serve the Lord with sincerity and integrity, fighting the good fight with a love for God's people will begin to receive the abundant resources necessary to perpetuate the gospel.

Having been faithful through all the trials, refusing to be moved from their stand on God's righteousness, they now will have the honor of being a part of a great outpouring of the Holy Spirit.

We have a great hope! When the children of Israel left Egypt they had a vision of hope, a promised destination. Jesus had a vision of hope that gave Him the determination to look beyond and endure the sufferings of the cross.

Likewise, we can look beyond our circumstances, our Red Sea crossings, our wilderness trials and obstacles. Yes, we can look beyond the Jordan River and the challenges that lie ahead. Our hope is in God!

We are living in some exciting yet intense times. As we follow the unfolding of world events, we are buffeted by a tidal wave of uncertainties that could cause some to despair. It's as if Luke 21 is happening before our eyes—the prophetic shakings and judgments of famines, pestilence, wars and rumors of wars.

Fortunately, verse 13 jumps out as an encouragement to us: "But it will turn out for you as an occasion for testimony" (NKJV). The inference is that the challenges and shakings we experience can become an opportunity for us to witness to others. We who have overcome by the blood of the Lamb and the word of our testimony (see Rev. 12:11) can use our trials to point multitudes to Jesus!

Leonard Ravenhill once sent me a note that literally still burns within my spiritual womb. "My dearest brother Doug," he wrote. "Let others live on the raw edge or the cutting edge…You and I should live on the edge of eternity."

After reading his note, I wrote these words as a constant reminder to me: "How can we settle into complacency while multitudes are in the balance of eternity? How can we be so hardened of heart as to sit back on the beach of comfort and apathy while so many are still shipwrecked in the sea of death?"

We hear about the cross so often that the thought of our sins putting Jesus there no longer breaks our hearts or ignites a burning passion of gratitude and service within us!

The fact is Jesus weeps over the needs of His people that are not being met. He weeps over the weary travelers who are struggling through the wilderness. He weeps over the millions who are lost without hope. It is because of His inestimable love that His ears are always open to our cry (see Ps. 34:19).

March 1999 Charisma

> "FROM A BARREN WOMB, THE LORD BROUGHT FORTH SAMUEL, THE FIRST OF A NEW GENERATION OF PROPHETS."

We have such a great opportunity before us to see a mighty harvest of changed lives! As Winkie Pratney writes in his book *Revival: Its Principles and Personalities,* "When God finds someone with courage to pray, preach, and live a life before Him of holiness and compassion, He can literally change the face of a nation."

The Lord wants each of us to leave a legacy to His glory. Regardless of our past mistakes or our present circumstances, He wants to birth through us a prophetic generation with a message of consecration, commitment and action.

It is time to cross our Jordans, to possess and occupy the land. God is ready to do His greatest work through each of us. It's time to push!

The Seed of Greatness

I believe the life of Hannah as recorded in 1 Samuel 1 offers a prophetic challenge and encouragement to the church at this time. Hannah was without child; her womb was barren. Yet out of her despair, misery, shame and pain, she cried out to God.

With desperate and passionate prayer she made a vow to the Lord: If He would give her a male child, she would commit her son to Him. God heard the cry of Hannah's heart and turned around what seemed to be an impossible situation. From a barren womb, the Lord brought forth Samuel, the first of a new generation of prophets.

God wants to turn crisis to victory, barrenness to greatness, in our lives, too. Regardless of our circumstances, the Lord wants to satisfy the longing in our souls. Though we may seem barren, with great odds stacked against us, He has placed his seed of greatness in every one of us who has called upon His name.

Discouragement, disappointments and distractions have caused some of us to forget the Lord's visions and dreams for us. But in each of our spiritual wombs is a seed of destiny waiting to be born.

There may be times of weeping and travailing between the porch and the altar (see Joel 2:17) prior to an outpouring or birthing of revival in our lives, but the Lord's promises are a sure foundation. A woman forgets her labor pains at the joy of holding her new child in her arms. Even as the prophet Eli spoke these words to Hannah as a promise to her, may each of us receive them as a promise of great things ahead: "Go in peace, and the God of Israel grant your petition which you have asked of Him" (1 Sam. 1:17). May we go from wilderness to victory from crisis to revival, from emptiness to greatness, from despair to joy. The time is now. Let's pray until something happens.

—Doug Stringer is founder of Somebody Cares America and Somebody Cares International, impacting communities through unified grassroots efforts.

Reprinted by permission Charisma Magazine and Strang Communications Company.

March 1999 Charisma

HOW TO FOLLOW GOD'S VOICE - IN INTERCESSION

LESSON 8

MY GOD WILL HEAR ME

MAIN PRINCIPLE

God wants us to pray the prayer of faith, with a solid vision of Him as our living and awesome God, who is waiting not only to hear, but also to grant our request.

HOW TO FOLLOW GOD'S VOICE - IN INTERCESSION

HEAR GOD'S VOICE

by Leonard LeSourd

Those of us who pray for others to be healed (James 5:14) can learn something from the amazing intercession work of Rees Howells, the Welsh coal miner. Rees never hesitated to pray for healings. But he depended totally on the Lord's direction as to the way he prayed.

How did a coal miner with limited education reach a spiritual level where he could hear the Lord's voice with regularity and obey it with certainty?

It came about because Rees had a hunger to know God and sought Him constantly through daily prayer. One day, at age 26, he heard this command: "Give your body to me that I may work through it. It must belong to me without reservation, for two persons with different wills can never live in the same body. If I come in as God, you must go out. I shall not mix Myself with your self."

Rees was stunned by this challenge of unconditional surrender—not unlike a sentence of death. He resisted for five days during which the contrast between the holiness of God and his own corrupt nature was starkly revealed. When Rees made the final surrender he was filled with the Holy Spirit and a ministry of power began. Shortly thereafter came one of the most difficult challenges of Rees' life.

Joe Evans, a dedicated helper and close friend, developed a severe case of tuberculosis. Doctors ordered him to a sanitarium. In agony of spirit, Rees sought the Lord for guidance. The answer came: *Let Joe follow medical advice.*

Five months in a sanitarium did not help, so the doctors suggested he try a tropical climate. "Was this right?" Rees asked the Lord. Again he was told to defer to the doctors.

Now Rees was faced with two dilemmas. First, Joe didn't have the money to go to a warmer climate. Second, if the money was available, there was no one in Joe's family to accompany him.

Several days later, Rees received a gift of 320 pounds sterling for his work, more than enough to handle a trip for two to a tropical location. Rees had no trouble turning this money over to his friend, but who would go with Joe? The Lord's next direction was devastating: *Do not ask someone else to do what you can do yourself.*

New studies had shown that TB (Britishers called it Consumption) was highly contagious. Since Rees was soon to be married, the possibility of contracting the disease filled him with horror. Yet did he have a choice? He and his fiancée agreed he did not.

In 1906 Rees Howells and Joe Evans traveled together to the island of Madeira in the Mediterranean. To save money, they stayed in a place called "The Sailor's Rest" provided by a Christian missionary. The food was terrible, vermin infested the place and the missionary was unfriendly.

Rees rebelled. "Lord, why this?" he prayed. There was no answer. Weeks passed and his anger toward the missionary grew. And there was no improvement in Joe. "I was tired and felt as if life wasn't worth living," Rees wrote in his journal. "I felt more like a man, than a man with the Holy Ghost inside me. I wanted to cry."

Rees was stricken. If the root of the Savior's nature was love, and if the root of his own nature was love, then nothing the missionary did could affect him. He was to love the missionary. The change that then occurred in Rees was dramatic.

Meanwhile, Joe was getting worse in the tropical climate, with both lungs nearly eaten away by the disease. Rees was afraid Joe was about to die when one day the Lord whispered gently to him: *A month from today, Joe will be restored.*

June 1985, Charisma

With jubilation Rees reported the news to Joe, the missionary and other friends. They looked at Rees as if he had lost his mind. But having this positive word from the Lord, Rees went ahead with complete faith. Boat reservations were made for the return to England a month later. Joyous letters were written to both families. The doctors involved shook their heads in dismay.

Though Joe's condition was unimproved, excitement grew in Rees and Joe as the day approached. When it finally came, Rees expected the healing to take place at dawn. Nothing happened. Instead, the Lord told Rees to announce in advance the good news to families back home by telegram. Another test of his faith, but Rees obeyed.

At noon, Joe and Rees were sitting in front of their lodgings when the Lord came down on Joe like a shower of rain. He was healed. It was instantaneous—so complete that Joe began to jump about and dance. Then he asked Rees to run a race with him. Then another. It seemed that all the Lord's power had gone to Joe's legs. It was joy unspeakable. Soon thereafter the two men made a triumphant return to Great Britain.

There are numerous lessons to learn from this story:
1. The Lord uses doctors and often will not act until a case is beyond medical help.
2. We can be His instruments for healing if we are willing to pay the price of surrender, self-discipline and obedience.
3. As we begin to pray for others, God will often do an unexpected work inside us.
4. The Lord does the healing at His choice of time and place.
5. The key to power in intercession is to learn to hear God's voice and then obey it.

—Leonard LeSourd (1919-1996) was an author, editor and publisher. He also co-founded the Intercessory Prayer Ministry. Some of his more popular books include *Touching The Heart Of God and Strong Men, Weak Men: Godly Strength and the Male Identity*.

Reprinted by permission Charisma Magazine and Strang Communications Company.

June 1985, Charisma

HOW TO FOLLOW GOD'S VOICE - IN INTERCESSION

AROUSE THYSELF TO PRAYER

by Mike Bickle

The Lord is calling us to be warriors in this hour. There is an urgency for the Army of God to become warriors.

One of the greatest qualities that distinguishes a good warrior from a poor warrior is the ability to stir himself up. This is also that which separates an ordinary combat man from a war hero. One can follow the commands of the General and the other stirs himself up to go beyond the normal service.

You are a blessed person if you have the ability to reach within yourself, get the engines moving, begin to take action and motivate yourself.

If there is an hour to be sleeping, this is not now. God is searching to and fro across the earth. He is looking for men and women that know how to stir themselves up in God that they might cross the line.

God says in Matthew 22:14, "Many are called but only a few chosen." Many are called but only a few cross the line. Only a few separate themselves and begin to discipline themselves that they might be equipped and chosen for the Army of God.

Is. 64:6-7 "For all of us have become like one who is unclean, and all our righteous deeds are like a filthy garment; and all of us wither like a leaf, and our iniquities, like the wind, take us away. And there is no one who calls on Thy name, who arouses himself to take hold of Thee: for Thou hast hidden Thy face from us, and has delivered us into the power of our iniquities."

TAKING HOLD OF GOD

"God has hidden His face" is Old Testament terminology meaning He has withheld His anointing. I believe God is saying today if we don't arouse ourselves and take hold of Him, the only other alternative is for us to be held captive by our own barrenness.

This is the hour we need to arouse ourselves. God is looking for hundreds and hundreds of soldiers right now. Stir yourself into action and lay hold of God.

Is. 52:1-2 "Awake, awake, clothe yourself in your beautiful garments, O Jerusalem, the holy city. For the uncircumcised and the unclean will no more come into you. Shake yourself from the dust, rise up, O captive Jerusalem; loose yourself from the chains around your neck, O captive daughter of Zion."

"Awake! Awake!" is the cry of God. We must get in the place where our faith will be made strong. This place is in God's presence which is prayer.

There are chains around the neck of the Church of Jesus Christ. The chains are only there because we have not aroused ourselves to take hold of the things of God. We must either cry out to God or find weeds growing in our garden.

We have chains around us but God is inviting us to lay the chains down. He has given us power and authority, but they only work if we live in the presence. God's power and authority never operates apart from God Himself. We have to be in contact with God to manifest His characteristics.

The end result of having God's power and authority without living in His presence is corruption. No man has the ability to keep his heart holy apart from God. If we don't have a prayer life, we are wide open for attacks from the devil.

LIVING ON YOUR KNEES

Don't get so busy that you quit living on your knees. The only place where holiness, love and humility are elevated is on our knees with the Word of God. If we don't have a prayer life, our strong desires for holiness are few. If we get ourselves out of the presence of God, we are destined to lose our desires for holiness, love and humility.

Romans 3:10-18 says that there is no one good; there is not one who seeks God apart from the grace of God. The only guarantee of loving God is keeping our knees bowed even when it's dry and barren in prayer.

Hebrews 7:16 "Who has become such, not on the basis of a law of physical requirement, but according to the power of an indestructible life."

This scripture describes a force, the power of an indestructible life as the eternal river that wells up in us. This eternal river is what keeps us moving in God.

If we quit contacting this river, our emotions are going to go backwards and we will begin to feel, sense and think the way we did even before we were saved. They get out of the place of the presence of God.

Isaiah says for us to stir ourselves up, loose our chains and break them. God's authority was never given to men to operate out of His presence. The Word of God only becomes alive when we are on our knees in God's presence. If we do not stir ourselves up to maintain a consistent prayer life, we are destined to lose our passion for holiness, love and humility. The authority of God will be an equation and a statement of fact and not a living reality to us.

The definition of "the ministry" is the ability to motivate and instruct people to touch God. If we can't pray, we won't have a ministry. Don't have a ministry made by man; have a ministry born in prayer. We must touch God in prayer and then teach others; otherwise, we will only cause confusion.

Too many like to get behind the pulpit because they like to stand in front of people for honor. Their chief goal is not to bring in the presence of God. If they wanted that with a passion, then they would be living out a more holy life themselves.

AWAKE IN HIS PRESENCE

This is an hour to awake. God will not allow His power and authority to become a reality in us until we live in His presence. He doesn't give His power apart from Himself. If we are not in love with Him, then His power will corrupt us. History shows it.

History is filled with generation after generation of people who started out in love with God, got too busy to stay on their knees, which is the highest point of arrogance, and then they fell.

Isaiah tells us to stand up and clothe ourselves in strength. How are we going to do it? There is only one way, by staying in God's presence.

Knowledge of the Word is step number one. It is absolutely essential. But knowledge of the Word without staying in His presence will not result in the release of God's power. It is only one of the 2 legs that we have to stand on. We have to also have knowledge of the Word. Yet again, that only becomes alive and quickened in us if we bow and live before Him in prayer.

Put on strength. How are we going to do this? Get in the Word and pray. Only from that will strength begin to flow from us.

SHAKING OURSELVES

There is a quality that we must cultivate: the ability to shake ourselves. We shouldn't wait until we are as barren as we can get before we finally wake up to the fact that we are dead in God. We need to shake ourselves from the dust or the things of this world. Then by laying hold of God, we will throw off the chains and things that are binding us. Walking with God is as easy as can be if we spend time in His presence. Everybody needs a prayer life. Everybody needs to be touching God. That is all that Christianity is. Christianity by definition is sharing life with God.

If we don't stir ourselves up, eventually circumstances will stir us. There is going to be a day and an hour when we are going to need the power of God flowing.

Loose yourselves from your chains. Live before God so that when things confront you, you will have the power and authority to break them. Don't wait until they come and then begin to cry out for power. Prayer is the best preventative medicine that can be put into our body.

We need to awake, clothe ourselves in strength, shake the dust off and loose the chains from around our necks.

In other words, set aside time to pray, put off the old things and get in the presence of God in prayer.

—Mike Bickle is the director of the International House of Prayer Missions Base of Kansas City and the author of several books including *Passion for Jesus, The Pleasures of Loving God,* and *Prayers to Strengthen Your Inner Man.* Mike's teaching emphasizes growing in passion for Jesus through intimacy with God.

Reprinted by permission: Equipping the Saints.

FOLLOWING GOD'S VOICE - IN INTERCESSION

THE POWER OF EARLY PRAYER

by Bob Bosworth

God has been speaking to me about prayer for a long time. I thought He wanted me to pray more, louder, harder or something. My desire to be obedient caused me to search the scriptures to understand His will.

This call to prayer came at a time in my life when it was necessary for my family and I to rise early, to meet the schedule of various members of my family. It also came during the time I was in the process of reading a book on Christian living which had a chapter on early rising. I became convinced for the first time, not from expediency, but from Scripture that it's God's will for His people to seek Him early every morning as a foundation for all we will learn and become as Christians.

As I studied the Scriptures, I found God's will plainly expressed concerning the necessity and desirability of beginning each day with early prayer and Bible study. The Song of Solomon 7:12 says:

"Let us get up early to the vineyards; let us see if the vine flourish, whether the tender grape appear, and the pomegranates bud forth: there will I give thee my loves."

This verse speaks of two things—first of fruitfulness and a relationship that exists between the bride, the Church, and the bridegroom, Jesus Christ, and that these two things are interrelated. You show me someone who looks over his life and is dissatisfied with his fruitfulness and I'll show you a case where the bride and the bridegroom don't know each other very well. There's a secret to fruitfulness which stems from a relationship with Christ. This relationship may survive through intermittent meetings during times of crisis, but it will not be the same as it is for the believer who greets Christ before the day has even begun.

Special Time

God has appointed a special time during which he wants to meet with His people. David found this out, especially when he wanted to find his way back into God's presence. He began to seek God even more fervently in the morning hours before dawn. David knew where and when to meet God. It's interlaced right into the whole of the Psalms. David was an early riser because he wanted to go out to greet His Lord.

"Awake up, my glory; awake, psaltery and harp: I myself will awake early. I will praise thee, O Lord, among the people: I will sing unto thee among the nations" (Psalm 57:8,9).

When did David give thanks and praise before the nations? Before church on Sunday? Before bed, when he had finished the day and was too tired to do anything else? He said, "I will awake right early," and you can too if you want to control the climate of your day. You can wake up early and sound off with a good chorus or with a hymn of praise. You can experience God just as David did in Psalm 63:1-4:

"O God thou art my God; early will I seek thee: my soul thirsteth for thee, my flesh longeth for thee in a dry and thirsty land, where no water is. To see thy power and thy glory, so as I have seen thee in the sanctuary. Because thy lovingkindness is better than life, my lips shall praise thee. Thus will I bless thee while I live: I will lift up my hands in thy name."

World Can't Scratch

We can call upon the Lord to "satisfy us early with thy mercy; that we may rejoice and be glad all our days" (Psalm 90:14). One of the things a Christian inherits is an eternal joy the world can't scratch—way down inside—the world can't get to it. Just as a woman said in my father's meeting years ago, "I have learned to be just as happy when I'm not happy as when I am!"

The secret to that kind of joy is being satisfied by the Lord in the morning, so Satan can't blow your day to smithereens before you enjoy the presence of the Lord.

We know Jesus knew this principle from the New Testament in Mark 1:35, "and in the morning, rising up a great while before day, he went out and departed into a solitary place, and there prayed." If the Creator of our world while He was veiled in the flesh knew how to seek the Father, shouldn't we follow His lead?

Proverbs 26:14 reflects Solomon's humor as well as his wisdom when he said, "As the door turneth upon its hinges, so doth the slothful upon his bed." If you love the Lord Jesus Christ more than you love your flesh or your bed, then you are going to get up and tell Him so. If you love your bed more than you love the Lord Jesus, you're going to stay put and let Solomon's description come into play. The pillow will feel so good on this side. Just like a door turning on its hinges, you may want to try the other side.

The scriptures I have quoted have had impact on my mind as I study other scriptures. Other principles have come into sharper focus, such as God's dealings with the children of Israel in the wilderness.

For forty years God fed His people with manna, but if you wanted to partake of the manna, you had to obey certain rules. The manna had to be collected very early in the morning because once the sun rose, it melted and you starved for the rest of the day. That's an important principle to learn, isn't it? The Church of Jesus Christ today remains in a semi-starved condition because they don't know what time to go collecting the gifts of love and mercy God wants to extend to us.

Are you a Christian who is living on yesterday's manna? Are you more self-sufficient than the King of Israel? This principle applies to every truth taught in the Bible. It applies to tithing just as it does to reading the Bible early in the morning. The Lord wants you to give your first fruit of your money and the first fruit of your day. If you received $10, went ahead and spent $9 of it and then gave $1 to the Lord, you wouldn't be tithing, because the tithe is the first fruit, not the last.

> WE ARE GOOD WATCHMEN OR BAD WATCHMEN, ACCORDING TO HOW WE OBEY THE RULES: BUT WE ARE WATCHMEN.

You should tithe your time in the same way you tithe your money. Studies in industry tell us the most productive time of a man's day is after he has had a good night's sleep, not when he's physically and mentally tired. If you intend to seek first the kingdom of God, you need to respect God like a boss who will tell you how to plan your day, before it's half over.

Be an Early Riser

We call Jesus "Lord," but is He Lord? If He is Lord, it seems that we would ask His will for our day, each day. Otherwise, there is no way we can know His will. We can hardly become backsliders if we arrange our lives and bedtimes to be pleasing to the Lord. We can shake the effects of affluency, of being part of a soft generation which lives at night, by scheduling our waking and sleeping according to God's plan, not what is on television or a party we just can't leave.

I believe God requires that we meet Him very early every morning if we expect a full anointing on our lives and ministry. Every great man of God in the Bible was an early riser—Abraham, Jacob, Moses, Joshua, Gideon, Hannah, Samuel, David, Job, all the apostles. One woman found a special place in the annals of God's dealings with man merely because she knew how to get up out of bed in the morning—Mary Magdalene was the first one to see the resurrected Christ!

Every great man throughout the history of the Christian Church has found this principle to be true. An examination of their biographies reveals that every one of them rose up early to spend time with the Lord. This practice used to be called the "morning watch." It fits in with what the Lord said, "Watch and pray, that you enter not into temptation: the spirit indeed is willing, but the flesh is weak" (Matthew 26:41). The men He said that to didn't pay attention and they denied their Lord. We should be what Ezekiel called "watchmen," and not of our country or of the people of our country, but the watchmen of the Lord. At any given time or place, it's the people of God who are watchmen for that time and place. We are good watchmen or bad watchmen, according to how we obey the rules: but we are all watchmen.

Watchmen Don't Sleep

A faithful watchman doesn't sleep while thieves steal his master's property. He is awake to stop the thief with all the power his master has bestowed upon him. This includes intercessory prayer for our family, friends and nation who will stumble and fall without help from God. Sometimes the Lord reminds us of this when we awake in the early morning hours with a burden on our heart for someone else. Sleep will only come after we have lifted up that person to the Lord.

Sometimes a person will ask me, "Well, what's the difference between an hour of prayer between 5 a.m. and 6 a.m. and between 11 a.m. and 12 noon? Mathematically there is no difference; one hour equals one hour, but spiritually there is no equation. Ask any man of God or try it yourself! It may require crucifying your nightlife, but you'll never regret it.

You can order your life to serve the Lord, if you will order it enough to rise before the sun to worship and pray; the rest will fall into place. The desire of your heart will be expressed as you rise up with the Lord. His will can be done in your life if you give Him the first fruit of the day.

—Bob Bosworth served as president and chief operating officer of Chattem, Inc., a subsidiary of Sanofi-Aventis until his retirement in 1972. He currently serves as Lead Independent Director of Covenant Transportation.

Reprinted by permission: Christ for the Nations.
CFNI, P.O.Box 769000, Dallas, TX 75376-9000, 800-933-2364

HOW TO FOLLOW GOD'S VOICE - IN INTERCESSION

LESSON 9

TRAVAILING AND PREVAILING INTERCESSION

MAIN PRINCIPLE

Effective travailing and prevailing prayer comes from belief in Jesus' words in Mark 11:24: ". . . Whatever you ask for in prayer, believe that you have received it, and it will be yours." Travailing and prevailing intercessors allow God to place His desire in their hearts and then continue praying in faith for God's desire, despite all obstacles, until it is established.

HOW TO FOLLOW GOD'S VOICE - IN INTERCESSION

ALL MANNER OF PRAYER

By Barbara Shull

God clearly admonishes, "Pray at all times—on every occasion, in every season—in the Spirit, with all (manner of) prayer and entreaty. To that end keep alert and watch with strong purpose and perseverance, interceding in behalf of all the saints (God's consecrated people)" (Eph. 6:18 TAB).

You can easily discern from the Amplified Bible that God wants you to pray constantly, and that you are to intercede with all manner of prayer. Sometimes your praying may be light and instantaneous. You might, while standing in line at the supermarket, sense the need of the customer in front of you and make a quick silent request of the Father on her behalf.

Or you may be visiting with a friend and discern that there is a truth in God's Word that she is not seeing clearly. Right then and there, eyes open, still involved in the conversation, you can pray, "God, please reveal Your truth to her. Thanks." This is one manner of prayer, and a very valid one.

There are many facets and levels of intercession, ranging from such spontaneous requests to strenuous travail. There are times when Jesus shares His heart of loving compassion with you and you actually identify with His heartbreak. This kind of praying may progress under the leading of the Spirit, into agonizing travail with weeping and deep groanings and may include manifestations such as muscle contractions. "Therefore are my (Isaiah's) loins filled with anguish; pangs have seized me like the pangs of a woman in childbirth; I am bent and pained so that I cannot hear, I am dismayed so that I cannot see" (Isa. 21:3 TAB). Very possibly this describes the travail that Jesus Himself experienced (Isa. 53:11). The interceding Holy Spirit is still inspiring this kind of travailing prayer in believers today.

The Apostle Paul describes another unusual type of intercession, sometimes but not always included in travail, one in which the Spirit "intercedes for us with groanings too deep for words" (Rom. 8:26 NASB).

Perhaps some of you are actually quenching the Holy Spirit and hindering His intercession by not allowing Him to release His heartbreaking cries to the Father through you. Sometimes you may experience strange feelings along with a constraint to plead to almighty God on behalf of another, but at the same time feel ashamed of being too emotional.

If this is the case, then you need to get alone with God and release these pent-up feelings, no matter what manifestations accompany your intercession. As you do, you will experience a rest and refreshing that enables you to continue your everyday business with greater efficiency because you are free from your inner burden. Since such intercession is a product of the Holy Spirit, you don't need to try to produce it. This beautiful and productive kind of prayer will simply come from deep within your innermost being.

Even though such travail and groaning is a valid form of prayer, remember that length, language, and emotional fervor do not determine the effectiveness of prayer. Jesus infers this in Matthew 6:5-8. Groaning in itself does not get answers; neither does weeping or travail. The kind of prayers that do get answers are those motivated by the Spirit of God. Whether intercession is lengthy or brief, prayed while on your knees or while driving the car, expressed matter-of-factly or with great passion, in English or other tongues, in high articulate language or unutterable groans, when inspired by the Holy Spirit, *it is effective!*

—Excerpted from Barbara Shull's book, *How to Become a Skilled Intercessor,* published by Women's Aglow Fellowship, Lynwood WA (now Aglow International, Edmonds WA).

Reprinted with permission from Women's Aglow Fellowship.

HOW TO FOLLOW GOD'S VOICE - IN INTERCESSION

TRAVAILING IN PRAYER

by Cindy Jacobs

Sometimes the Lord places us in unusual circumstances to illustrate for us a principle of kingdom living.

When the editors of *Charisma* asked me to write a column about travailing prayer, I didn't have a clue about how I would start. Then, as I prayed, I sensed the Lord's gentle voice saying, "Tell them about Brynne."

Brynne Alexis Morris was born on December 29, 1993, after a long, difficult labor. Her mom and dad, David and Laurie lead worship at our church. They had received a number of rather dire reports about this baby.

On the day Brynne was born, I was praying in the morning in the birthing room. As Laurie underwent serious labor pangs, I sat in a rocking chair praying for her and the baby.

Things didn't bode well for this child. The doctors said there was meconium in the amniotic fluid—a serious medical problem.

As I prayed quietly, I sensed a terrific warfare in the heavenlies. Deep within my spirit, I groaned.

At times I bound the spirit of death, which seemed like a thick cloud in the room. While Laurie and Brynne travailed together during the birth process, I travailed in prayer.

Despite the intensity of the spiritual battle, I sensed God's victory and that the baby would be born whole. Finally, after long hours of contractions, little Brynne was born—a beautiful, healthy little girl.

I wonder if those of us who prayed for little Brynne were experiencing something of what the apostle Paul described in Galatians 4: "My little children, for whom I am again suffering birth pangs until Christ is completely and permanently formed (molded) within you" (v. 19, Amp.). Although Paul was not specifically talking about intercessory prayer in this passage, I believe it's safe to assume he travailed in prayer for the Galatians.

> TRAVAILING PRAYER IS A WORK OF THE HOLY SPIRIT, NOT SOMETHING WE MANUFACTURE.

What exactly is *travailing prayer?* Travailing prayer is strong intercession that can be likened to labor pangs. It is prevailing prayer that helps "give birth" to God's will in a crucial situation. Travailing prayer is a work of the Holy Spirit, not something we manufacture.

The intensity of the intercession is not necessarily marked by loud praying. Though there are times when Christians may weep or groan aloud when praying, it's possible to do this inwardly without making a sound.

For instance, it wouldn't have been beneficial to David and Laurie if I had started groaning on the birthing room floor. In this situation the Spirit led me to intercede inwardly in a way that was just as intense and effective.

At other times I have cried aloud as I travailed in prayer. One Wednesday night at church, I deeply felt a leading from the Lord to weep and travail for Cuba. Though we hadn't been talking about or praying for Cuba, I knew God wanted to revive and release that nation.

It wouldn't have been appropriate for me to enter into travail in that service, so I told my husband, Mike: "Honey, I have to go home and pray for Cuba." In the quiet of my home, tears poured from my eyes as I cried loudly to the Lord for a spiritual breakthrough.

May 1994, Charisma

When God calls us to travail, it's important to remember that He is a God of order. There are those who make themselves moan and groan loudly, but the groaning of God's Spirit in prayer is not something that can be turned off and on like a faucet.

I have seen churches where the people writhe on the floor every Sunday to pray over any request. Often the people are so loud they could not possibly pray in agreement with the person leading the intercession. Though some of that activity may have been inspired by the Hoy Spirit, I know the call to travail will not come upon every person every week.

Just because there are some excesses, however, we should not throw the baby out with the bathwater. Travailing prayer is a valid and powerful expression of Spirit-led intercession. We simply need to be careful that we don't let our emotions run wild.

Many reading this column may be suffering from discouragement. Some are heartbroken over a wayward spouse or child. Others are standing on the brink of disaster surrounded by impossible circumstances.

Let me encourage you to give the Lord the liberty to teach you about travailing prayer. Such powerful intercession can bring a breakthrough if you don't give up!

We live in exciting times when God is calling many of us to pray for His kingdom to come in the lives of our families and in the nations of the earth. Let us pray until Christ is formed in us—and until the nations experience His kingdom power.

—Cindy Jacobs is a respected prophet who travels the world ministering not only to crowds of people, but also to heads of nations. Cindy has authored several books, including *Possessing the Gates of the Enemy, The Voice of God* and *The Power of Persistent Prayer*. Cindy loves to travel and speak, but one of her favorite pastimes is spending time with her husband Mike, two grown children and their adorable grandchildren.

Reprinted by permission Charisma Magazine and Strang Communications Company

May 1994, Charisma

FOLLOWING GOD'S VOICE - IN INTERCESSION

WHY IS IT SO HARD FOR CHRISTIANS TO PRAY?

by David Wilkerson

I've been perplexed for some time about a problem that has persisted in the church for years and it concerns me deeply. The problem is, why is it so hard for Christians to pray?

Scripture makes it clear that the answer to everything in our lives is prayer mixed with faith. The apostle Paul writes, "Be careful [anxious] for nothing; but in every thing by prayer and supplication with thanksgiving let your requests be made known unto God" (Philippians 4:6). Paul is telling us, "Seek the Lord about every area of your life. And thank him ahead of time for hearing you!"

Paul's emphasis is clear: Always pray first! We aren't to pray as a last resort going to our friends first, then to a pastor or counselor, and finally ending up on our knees. No, Jesus tells us, "Seek ye first the kingdom of God, and his righteousness; and all these things shall be added unto you" (Matthew 6:33). We're to go to the Lord first before anyone!

It's heartrending to read the letters sent to our ministry from multitudes of broken Christians. Families are breaking up, spouses are divorcing, people who walked faithfully with Christ for years are living in fear and defeat. Each of these people has been overcome by something—sin, depression, worldliness, covetousness. And year after year, their problems only seem to get worse.

Yet, what shocks me most about their letters is that very few of these Christians ever mentions prayer. They turn to tapes, books, counselors, call-in shows, therapies of all kinds but rarely ever to prayer. They go through each day worrying, fretting, living with a cloud hanging over their heads, because they don't have an answer to their problems.

Why is it so hard for Christians, in times of crisis, to seek God for their desperate needs? After all, the Bible stands as one long testimony that God hears the cries of his children and answers them with tender love:

- "The eyes of the Lord are upon the righteous, and his ears are open unto their cry" (Psalm 34:15).
- "The righteous cry, and the Lord heareth, and delivereth them out of all their troubles" (verse 17).
- "This is the confidence that we have in him, that, if we ask any thing according to his will, he heareth us: and if we know that he hear us, whatsoever we ask, we know that we have the petitions that we desired of him" (1 John 5:14-15).
- "...The effectual fervent prayer of a righteous man availeth much" (James 5:16).
- "All things, whatsoever ye shall ask in prayer, believing, ye shall receive" (Matthew 21:22).
- "...the prayer of the upright is his delight" (Proverbs 15:8).
- "The Lord...heareth the prayer of the righteous" (verse 29).
- "He will regard the prayer of the destitute, and not despise their prayer" (Psalm 102:17).

Listen to David's great boast: "In the day when I cried thou answeredst me, and strengthenedst me with strength in my soul" (138:3). David said, "I've proven you, God! In all my trials, I turned to no one else. I sought only you—and you heard me, answered me, and gave me strength for the battle I was facing!" "Thou calledst in trouble, and I delivered thee; I answered thee..." (81:7).

These promises and testimonies are overwhelming evidence of God's care. And they're so varied, profound and numerous, I don't understand how any Christian could miss them!

Yet when it comes to prayer, the Bible gives us more than promises. It also gives us warnings about the danger of neglecting prayer: "How shall we escape, if we neglect so great salvation..." (Hebrews 2:3). The Greek word for "neglect" here means "of little concern; to take lightly."

The context of this verse is a discussion of things related to our salvation—and prayer is obviously one of these. God is asking, "How do you expect to escape ruin and devastation in the dark times coming, if you haven't learned to commune with me in prayer? How will you know and recognize my voice in that day, if you haven't learned to hear it in your secret closet?"

I believe God is deeply wounded by the neglect of prayer among his people today. Jeremiah writes: "Can a maid forget her ornaments, or a bride her attire? Yet my people have forgotten me days without number" (Jeremiah 2:32).

Here is my big question—the one thing I simply cannot understand: How can God's own people—who are under constant attack from hell, facing trouble and temptations on all sides go—week after week without ever seeking him? And how can they claim to love him and believe in his promises, yet never draw near to his heart?

The Writer of Hebrews Calls Us to "Draw Near to God"!

Hebrews 10 contains an incredible promise. It says God's door is always open to us, giving us total access to the father:

"Having therefore, brethren, boldness to enter into the holiest by the blood of Jesus, by a new and living way, which he hath consecrated for us, through the veil, that is to say, his flesh; and having an high priest over the house of God; let us draw near with a true heart in full assurance of faith, having our hearts sprinkled from an evil conscience, and our bodies washed with pure water" (Hebrews 10:19-22).

A few verses later, we're warned the day of the Lord is fast approaching: "Not forsaking the assembling of ourselves together, as the manner of some is; but exhorting one another: and so much the more, as ye see the day approaching" (verse 25). God is saying, "Even now, as the time of Christ's return draws closer, you must seek my face. It's time to go into your secret closet and get to know me!"

I believe were already seeing the signs that prove we're close to a meltdown of our financial system: Violence and immorality are on the rise. Our society is pleasure mad. False prophets—"angels of light"— have already deceived many with their doctrines of demons. And, at any time, we can expect to see the hour of tribulation, which will cause men's hearts to fail with fear. Yet, before all this happens, the writer of Hebrews says:

"Don't let the truth slip away from you! Stay awake and alert. You have an open door into God's holy presence—so, go into him with full assurance of faith, making your petitions known. Christ's blood has already made the way for you—and nothing stands between you and the father. You have every right to enter into the holy of holies, to receive all the help you need!"

When we take lightly Jesus' sacrifice—which he gave so we could have access to the father for all our needs—we "do despite" to the grace of God, provoking his anger!

Yet, even with all these powerful warnings about the dangers of neglecting prayer, Christians still find it hard to pray. Why? I believe there are four reasons for this:

1. **Some Christians Don't Pray Because They Have a Lukewarm Love for the Lord!**

When I use the word "lukewarm" to describe a person's love for Jesus, I don't mean he's cold toward the Lord. Rather, I mean his love is "inexpensive"—not costly. Let me give you an example:

When Jesus addresses the church at Ephesus in Revelation 2, he first commends them for all they've done. He acknowledges they've labored hard in the faith—hating sin and compromise, refusing to accept false doctrines, never fainting or giving up when persecuted, always taking a stand for the gospel.

But, Christ says, he holds one thing against them: They've forsaken their fervent, expensive love for him! "Nevertheless I have somewhat against thee, because thou hast left thy first love" (Revelation 2:4).

Somehow amid all their good works, they left behind their loving, disciplined walk with Jesus. And now he tells them, "You've left your first love. You've forsaken the costly discipline of coming into my presence, to commune with me!"

Please note: Jesus is speaking here of believers who started out with a burning love for him. He isn't addressing dead, cold, nominal Christians, who never loved him in the first place. Rather, he's saying, "It's possible for someone who once had a heart of love for me to let his zeal become lukewarm. The devoted servant who once ran daily to seek me in his secret closet now seldom prays at all!"

Think about how insulting this must be to Christ, who is our bridegroom. What kind of marriage can there be when a husband and wife have no private times of intimacy? And that's just what Jesus is talking about here. He wants moments with you all to himself, to enjoy intimacy!

You may say you love him—but if you never show up to be with him, you prove you don't love him at all. That kind of behavior would never cut it with another lover. If you told your girlfriend you loved her, but you only saw her once a week—just long enough to say, "Hi, honey, I love you, now goodbye!"—she wouldn't put up with it. Why should Jesus, who gave his all—his very life—for you?

It doesn't matter how loudly you praise the Lord in church, how much you say you love him, how many tears you shed. You can give generously, love others, hate sin, rebuke wrongdoers—but if your heart isn't being continually drawn to Christ's presence, you simply don't love him. You're taking prayer lightly, neglecting it—and, according to Jesus' own words, that's proof you've lost your love for him.

All our works are in vain, unless we return to our bright-burning love for Jesus. We have to realize, "Loving Jesus isn't just about doing things. It involves the daily discipline of maintaining a relationship. And that will cost me something!"

2. Some Christians Don't Pray Because They've Perverted Their Priorities!

A priority is the importance you place on something. And Christians who neglect prayer have perverted their priorities! Many believers pledge they'll pray if and when they can find the time. Yet each week, seeking Christ becomes less important to them than washing the car, cleaning the house, visiting friends, eating out, going shopping, watching sports. They simply don't make time to pray.

Yet people were no different in the days of Noah and Lot. Their top priorities were eating and drinking, buying and selling, marrying and caring for their families. They had no time to listen to messages of God's coming judgment. And so no one was prepared when judgment fell!

Evidently, nothing has changed over the centuries. For most Americans, God remains at the bottom of the priority list. And at the top are income, security, pleasure, family. Of course, for many Americans God doesn't even make the list. But that doesn't grieve the Lord nearly as much as how little he's valued by his own children!

Today, thousands of Christians are traveling across the country just to be prayed over by some minister, prophet or evangelist. These believers want to feel God's touch and have some ecstatic experience of his presence. But even if they get what they're looking for, the experience only lasts a short time. And, ironically, the whole time they're traveling and seeking God's touch, they don't spend five minutes in prayer!

Beloved, the Lord doesn't want your leftovers—those little bits and pieces of time when you have only a moment to toss up a quick prayer request. That isn't a sacrifice of prayer. It's a lame offering—and it pollutes his altar!

The prophet Malachi writes: "If ye offer the blind for sacrifice, is it not evil? And if ye offer the lame and sick, is it not evil? Offer it now unto thy governor; will he be pleased with thee, or accept thy person? saith the Lord of hosts" (Malachi 1:8).

Malachi is saying, "You're bringing just any old farm animals to sacrifice in God's presence. But these are careless, thoughtless, secondhand gifts. Try giving those kinds of offerings to your governor. He'd have you thrown out of his presence!"

God expected his people to go through their flocks carefully, examining every animal, to choose the most perfect specimen among them for sacrifice to him. And likewise today, God expects the same from us. He wants our quality time—time that wont be rushed or hurried. And we're to make that time a priority!

I once met with the pastor of one of America's largest churches. This man was one of the busiest ministers I'd ever seen. He told me without apology, "I have no time to pray." Yet, what he really meant was, "I don't give any priority to prayer."

When I visited his church, I sensed no moving of God's Spirit in the congregation. In fact, it was one of the deadest churches I'd ever preached in. Yet, how could there be any life, if the pastors didn't pray?

The fact is, no Christian will set aside time to pray unless it becomes his first priority in life, above everything else above family, career, leisure time, everything. Otherwise, his sacrifice is perverted!

3. Some Christians Don't Pray Because They've Learned to Live Without Prayer!

Many Christians think all that's required of them is to go to church, worship, listen to the preaching, resist sin, do their very best, and all will be well for them. This is the sacrifice they bring to God—and they think he's pleased with it!

I've spent time at the bedsides of dying Christians who were faithful churchgoers for over fifty years. These people never missed a meeting. They were good, family people, and they could talk about every spiritual subject. But they had no prayer life whatsoever. They spent hours with their family, or sitting in front of a TV, or working on their hobbies—but they had no time to be alone with Christ.

This may sound harsh to you, but I believe those people went into eternity not knowing their Lord. God never drew near to them—because they never drew near to him!

I fear for every Christian who's learned to live comfortably with no daily prayer life—who's never had a growing communion with the Lord. Such people end up strangers to him. And they'll be among those whom Christ rebukes on judgment day: "Yes, you did many great works—you healed people, you performed miracles, you brought many into my kingdom. But I never knew you. Depart from me, stranger!"

How can we escape God's anger and displeasure, if we neglect his great gift of salvation? How can we face him on judgment day, when the books are opened to reveal we haven't spent any time with him? We may answer, "Lord, I realize I made very little time for you. I spent it all on myself, my family, my career. But now I'm ready to spend eternity getting to know you." Do you think he'll stand for that? No—never!

The fact is, you can easily spend a whole lifetime without prayer. In fact, I know of some very "successful" pastors and evangelists who've to learned to minister completely without prayer. They can entertain you, tell you great stories and make you laugh. But they can't convict you, change you, or move you to seek God's face!

After a while, these men fall into deep despair. Why? They become more and more dependent on the arm of the flesh, rather than on the Lord. And their lives become full of confusion on every side. Prayerless preachers are powerless preachers!

Likewise, prayerless Christians are shallow in their faith, easy targets for false teachers, quickly led astray from the true gospel. Such Christians are always "learning"—but never maturing!

4. Some Christians Don't Pray Because They Don't Believe God Hears Their Prayers!

Over time, many believers get discouraged over unanswered prayers—and, finally, they simply give up. They think, "Maybe I just lack faith. All I know is, prayer doesn't work for me. And why should I pray if it doesn't work?"

The Israelites in Isaiah's time had the same attitude. Isaiah wrote: "They seek me daily, and delight to know my ways, as a nation that did righteousness...they ask of me...they take delight in approaching to God. Wherefore have we fasted, say they, and thou seest not? Wherefore have we afflicted our soul, and thou takest no knowledge [notice]?..." (Isaiah 58:2-3).

These people were accusing God of child neglect! They were saying, "I love God—I do right and avoid sin. And, until recently, I've been faithful to seek him in prayer. But, you know what? He's never answered me! So, why should I continue afflicting my soul before him? He's never taken notice of my pleadings!"

Many unmarried Christian women tend to think this way. They say, "For years I've sought the Lord sincerely, asking him to bring a godly man into my life. I've prayed for over a decade now. But nothing has happened! "So they try to make a marriage happen on their own—and disaster follows.

Recently, a pastor wrote an alarming letter to me. He said: "Brother Wilkerson, this past week I shut down the church I've pastored for several years. I simply disbanded the congregation and left the pulpit. For years we prayed for revival—but it never happened. We prayed for a building—but it never came through. Over the years, we dwindled to thirty people. It just wasn't working. And now I'm leaving to find another job."

I pity this dejected man. Yet, I agree— he needs another job, because he probably wasn't called to ministry in the first place. You see, our calling isn't to see revival happen, to have a church building, or to have respectable numbers in the congregation. No—it's to minister to the Lord faithfully—and that includes our prayer life!

James writes that God doesn't answer the prayers of those who ask for things simply to satisfy themselves: "Ye ask, and receive not, because ye ask amiss, that ye may consume it upon your lusts" (James 4:3). In other words: "You're not asking for God's will. You're not ready to submit to whatever he wants. Rather, you're trying to dictate to him those things that will satisfy your own heart!"

Make no mistake—our God is utterly faithful. Paul writes, "...let God be true, but every man a liar..." (Romans 3:4). He's saying, in essence, "It doesn't matter if you hear a million voices crying, 'Prayer doesn't work. God doesn't hear me!' Let every man be called a liar. God's word stands—and he is faithful to hear us!"

Jesus said, "...whatsoever ye shall ask in prayer, believing, ye shall receive" (Matthew 21:22). Simply put, Christ is saying, "If you truly believe, you'll be willing to wait and expect an answer from your heavenly father. And it won't matter to you how long it takes. You'll hold on in faith, believing he'll answer!"

If God has delayed answering a particular prayer of yours, you can be sure he's testing your faith.

He wants you to trust him when he appears to be silent. And he tests you, to see if you'll say, "I give up. He doesn't answer!" Ultimately, he wants your faith to come forth as pure as gold—so you'll be equipped to receive many answers, both for you and for others!

I once read the story of a godly saint—a dear, older sister who'd walked closely with Jesus for many years. Her prayer life was so strong, people everywhere asked her to pray for them. One day a friend wrote to her asking for prayer, and the woman agreed.

A few weeks later, this godly woman received another letter from that same friend, saying, "Thank you for praying—I've been healed!" But the godly woman realized she'd forgotten to pray! She rejoiced that her friend had been healed—yet she wondered, "Lord, she said her faith was weak. Why did you heal her, if I forgot to pray?"

God answered her: "I healed her because you've gotten to know me! You've grown so close to me, I fulfilled the very desire you had for your friend—even without your prayer."

"Oh how great is thy goodness, which thou hast laid up for them that fear thee; which thou hast wrought for them that trust in thee before the sons of men!" (Psalm 31:19). "...they that seek the Lord shall not want any good thing" (34:10).

Go to your secret closet regularly, and seek him with all your heart. That's your answer to a healed marriage, to unsaved family members, to every need in your life. Your answers may not come overnight. Yet, God will do his work in his time and his way. Your part is to believe he is faithful to answer—because you're his beloved child!

—David Wilkerson was the founding pastor of Times Square Church in New York City. There he ministered to gang members and drug addicts. In 1971, he founded World Challenge, Inc., which supports missionaries and outreaches throughout the world. He died in 2011.

Reprinted by permission: World Challenge, Inc., P.O. Box 260, Lindale, TX75771.
http://worldchallenge.org.

HOW TO DONATE TO ZOE MINISTRIES

Help us deliver the message of Life throughout the World!

In addition to providing support for ZOE missions, curriculum development/translation and course scholarships, many of our translated materials will be donated to believers without resources to purchase them.

Would you prayerfully consider supporting this ministry?

YOU ARE ABLE TO MAKE A DONATION IN ANY OF THE FOLLOWING WAYS:

Online with a Credit Card
Visit our website to make a secure online donation.
www.zoeministries.org/donate/

By Automatic Bill Pay
Recurring donations to ZOE or to a designated ZOE missionary may be set up with your bank.

By Check
Please make checks payable to 'ZOE Ministries International'
Our Address is – PO Box 2207, Arvada, CO 80001-2207, U.S.A.

May God bless you richly for your support of this ministry!

"Now this is eternal life [zoe]: that they may know you, the only true God, and Jesus Christ, whom you have sent." - John 17:3

LESSON 10

INTERCESSION OF PAUL

MAIN PRINCIPLE

We can look at Paul's example and gain a pattern of prayer for our own lives. Paul's prayers reveal the depth of relationship he maintained with the Lord. Paul received much from God, and he desired that the people for whom he labored would also receive abundantly.

HOW TO FOLLOW GOD'S VOICE - IN INTERCESSION

I INTERCEDED IN THE SPIRIT DURING MY 'PRAYER DREAMS'

by Pauline Harthern

I've always known that God never sleeps. He cares for His children 24 hours a day. But I never thought God could use *me* 24 hours a day, that is, not until I had some remarkable dreams.

The first dream occurred in January of 1976. Roy and I were in Acapulco, Mexico, celebrating our 25th wedding anniversary and also enjoying the honeymoon which we had never had.

We looked forward to time in the surf and catching up on reading. When we unpacked our suitcases, we discovered we'd left all those books we intended to read back home in our bedroom. We looked through the hotel lobby. Everything was in Spanish except for the *New York Time—* which was $3.75 per copy.

It seemed the Lord intended for us to stick with His Word—rather than men's words. Roy found a bilingual Gideon Bible in the hotel room, and I spent the time with my pocket New Testament. The long hours with the Bible gave us a tremendous feeling of exhilaration—not only spiritually but emotionally and physically as well.

One night as I drifted off to sleep with the Word of God, I dreamed of Roy's secretary, Ruth, from a former church. She was in great distress.

In the dream I linked my arm through hers, and we began praying in the Spirit as we climbed a difficult mountain. We both became exhausted and were tempted to quit. Yet we kept on praying—kept on climbing.

On arriving at the summit, gasping and faint, I sensed a great feeling of victory. She felt it too. We held each other in sheer ecstasy, rejoicing.

The next morning I told my husband of the dream, wondering if Ruth might be in some kind of distress. "Even in my dream I felt I should pray for her," I said.

We finished the conversation and continued vacationing.

January 1983, Charisma

However, on coming home from our trip, I found, in my stack of mail, clippings from the Jacksonville, Florida newspaper. The apartment complex where Ruth's daughter lived alone had been invaded by a maniac who entered other apartments also, attacking and killing the occupants. He had returned to Ruth's daughter's apartment several times. Each time he was unable to gain entrance although the lock to her door was the same as all the other locks where he had entered.

It seemed he had been supernaturally restrained. Could it be that the Holy Spirit had actually prayed through me, even through I was asleep? I remembered Song of Solomon 5:2, "I was asleep, but my heart was awake" (NAS).

Was my "unconscious" prayer part of the reason the girl had been protected from evil? It was an exciting question.

Then, four years later, I had another "prayer dream." In the dream a dear friend came to me and said, "Pauline, Jim is dying." A genteel lady, Mary Lou, stood silently wringing her hands and biting her lips to keep from crying. In my dream I began to pray, pacing the floor, rebuking death, binding the enemy, and praying in the Spirit. The "prayer dream" seemed to last for hours until suddenly I just felt "good" all over.

> IT SEEMED THE ATTACKER HAD BEEN SUPERNATURALLY RESTRAINED. COULD IT BE THAT THE HOLY SPIRIT HAD ACTUALLY PRAYED THROUGH ME, EVEN THOUGH I WAS ASLEEP?

"It's all right." I assured Mary Lou.

The next morning, Sunday, I again told my husband what had happened. "It seems I battled all night for Jim."

Roy reminded me our friend was scheduled for open heart surgery later in the week.

We arrived at the church early that morning, just as one of the elders pulled up in his car. His face was haggard. He had been up all night.

"We almost lost Jim last night," he said.

"But he doesn't have surgery until later this week," I exclaimed.

"Oh no, he had it last night. Something went terribly wrong, but he's fine now."

I knew I was not the only one who had been praying for Jim, but I was again startled over the method the Holy Spirit had used to pray through me. It had been another "prayer dream."

Last month it happened again. In my dream I was in Europe visiting a pastor and his wife, dear friends of ours who minister in a capital city.

As I chatted with them, one by one their four daughters came in. I marveled at their growth and beauty. All were happily serving the Lord.

Suddenly the oldest girl left the room. I sensed she was deeply disturbed and followed her.

Roy appeared in my dream, and I said to him, "We must pray for Elizabeth. She seems to be very burdened." I began to intercede.

After I awoke the next morning, Elizabeth remained in my thoughts and prayers. The burden lasted all day, and then disappeared. The following week the European pastor called. He was in the States and wanted to have lunch.

"Your daughters are just beautiful," I said to his astonishment. I teased him a little by saying I had seen them all just a week before.

Then I became serious and told him of my dream and also my concern for Elizabeth.

The Pastor's voice became serious. "Our girls are all happily serving the Lord, but a lot has happened to Elizabeth. She has been very troubled not knowing which direction to go. She has many decisions to make in the near future. Surely your prayer dream was directed by God."

We continued our conversation, but I couldn't help reflecting on the strange way God had used me to intercede.

God really does work in mysterious ways. And what seems odd in the natural may be quite normal in the spiritual.

God can't be put in our little boxes. Paul's words in Romans 11:33 are true: "How unsearchable are God's judgments, and his ways past finding out!"

I do not understand most of my dreams. But the Spirit of God who never sleeps has given me special understanding of these three.

Perhaps there will be others. I hope so. For what could be more assuring than to realize that the Holy Spirit has me busy interceding for my friends—not only when I am awake but also as I sleep.

—Pauline Harthern was an author and teacher. Her more popular books include *Miracles From My Diary, From Tragedy to Triumph* and *Speaking Creative Words*. She and her husband, Roy, pastored several churches in the U.S., most recently Calvary Assembly of God in Winter Park, FL. Ms. Harthern passed away at age 90 in 2020.

Reprinted by permission Charisma Magazine and Strang Communications Company.

January 1983, Charisma

HOW TO FOLLOW GOD'S VOICE - IN INTERCESSION

LESSON 11

GOD IS SEARCHING FOR INTERCESSORS

MAIN PRINCIPLE

Intercession is foundational to action, and action completes intercession. As we seek God's direction and pray, we must follow through in obedience and be willing to carry out God's plans

HOW TO FOLLOW GOD'S VOICE - IN INTERCESSION

THIS PRAYER GROUP IS DRIVING ME CRAZY

by Eddie Smith

INTERCESSORS HAVE A SPECIAL CALL, BUT THE INSIGHTS THEY RECEIVE IN PRAYER SOMETIMES CAN CAUSE PROBLEMS. WATCHFUL SHEPHERDS MUST BRING NEEDED ACCOUNTABILITY WITHOUT HARMFUL CONTROL.

A couple of years ago, a man invited me to lunch to ask for my advice. "My pastor has asked me to become prayer coordinator for our church," he said, "Tell me, what should I do first?"

"Go back and resign," I told him.

Not used to my dry humor, he was taken aback. "Resign? Why?"

"It's a dumb thing he wants you to do."

"What do you mean?" he asked.

"Your pastor more than likely wants you to take the church directory and divide the names into prayer groups of 15," I explained. "Then he wants you to select a prayer captain to be over each group and a prayer coordinator to be over every three captains."

The man took out a pen and began to write furiously.

"Wait a minute," I said. "What are you doing?"

"Getting all this down," he said without looking up.

"But I already told you: It's a dumb idea," I said, laughing. "That's not a prayer ministry; it's multilevel recruiting! You'll not be pastoring prayer; you'll spend all your time managing 'the machine.'"

It's sad but true: For too long we pastors have invested the bulk of our time trying to squeeze prayer out of the 90 percent of the church who are not going to pray while neglecting the 10 percent of the church who have a heart to pray. Let's face it. We are never going to motivate all our members to be prayer warriors.

I told my lunch partner, "Go back to your pastor and tell him you'll pastor the praying people in the church. Conduct a survey. Find out who they are. List them, enlist them, love them, and pour your heart into them. You'll discover that, like rabbits, they will multiply on you!"

A STRATEGIC PARTNERSHIP

In fact, explosive multiplication is taking place all over the world today as more and more believers are sensing an urgent call to pray. God, it seems, is calling His watchmen to the towers and His gatekeepers to the gates. Intercessors, as God's "watchmen," are discovering their call and assuming their positions.

Some observers estimate the global altar of prayer is now 180 million intercessors strong—and counting. Coordinated by more than 1,500 national and international prayer networks, these committed prayer warriors are serious about the completion of the Great Commission, and they know prayer is the key to success.

Meanwhile, many of us who are pastors—the "gatekeepers"—are trading our past competition with and suspicion of these "strange prayer people" for strategic partnerships and highly energized and effective prayer groups.

While most pastors (hopefully) are seasoned and disciplined "prayers," few are intercessors. Our primary gift is the pastoral ministry and not the other solitary, time-intensive ministry of intercessory prayer.

April 1987, Charisma

As a result, many of us haven't understood intercessors or the ministry of intercession. But a growing number of us are learning.

We're coming to understand that intercession, like pastoring, is a valid ministry and that every intercessor is a minister. (Bill Bright has said he hopes one day to be promoted from president of Campus Crusade for Christ to the office of intercessor!) And we're learning to partner with our intercessors—even as the Old Testament gatekeepers partnered with the watchmen atop the city walls.

Though most of us see "ministry" as going to people *for* God, intercession is going to God *for* people—and that's what makes it a critical function. Intercession is foundational to every other ministry of the church. Unless bathed in prayer, other ministries are like cut flowers: They may look and smell good for a season, but in time they fade and die.

As intercessors do their part, others in the body of Christ can do theirs. Pastors, for example, do not have to perform ministry alone. While we develop our own prophetic gifts and abilities, we can identify and partner with those in our churches who have revelatory gifts and spiritual discernment. They are the "eyes and ears" of the body, making them an important part of the whole.

All intercessors, of course, are not alike. They come in a great variety and can be both complicated and delightful people. As a pastor, I've found them exciting and invigorating to be around—not to mention challenging. Because intercessors are often passionate, aggressive people, pastoring them can be a bit intimidating.

> "INTERCESSORS ARE GOD'S SPIRITUAL ACTIVISTS. THEY ARE DRIVEN NOT TO THE STREETS WITH PLACARDS BUT TO THE PRAYER CLOSET WITH WEEPING AND TRAVAIL."

But pastors who are willing to be open to them find that most often the intercessors are some of the most informed, envisioned people in their congregation. They are God's spiritual activists. That's because they live with what I call a "holy dissatisfaction." Essentially discontented with the status quo, they're driven not to the streets with placards and slogans, but to the prayer closet with weeping and travail.

Pastors can understand this because we experience similar tensions. We live with the joy, the frustration and sometimes the crushing weight of leadership. Both intercessors and pastors are burden-bearers. They bear not only their own burdens but also the burdens of others, as well as the burden of the Lord. In this, we're on common ground.

PASTORING INTERCESSORS

From talking with intercessors worldwide, I can say to pastors without hesitation: Our intercessors need us—and they want to be pastored! But few of us really know how to properly and effectively shepherd people who have the gift of intercession. How can we do this?

1. **Identify them.** We can't effectively pastor intercessors if we don't know who they are! And the fact is they may not know who they are either; they may be people of prayer, but they may not know that their sense of prayer urgency is actually a gift from God.

    We must help them discover their calling. One way: Survey your church membership using the spiritual gifts test in C. Peter Wagner's classic, *Your Spiritual Gifts Can Help Your Church Grow*, published by Regal Books.

2. **Instruct them.** Properly taught, prayer warriors are a powerful weapon in the arsenal of the church (supposing we make use of the weapons at our disposal). In addition to solid biblical teaching about prayer and spiritual warfare, they need to learn "skills" that are important in working with other ministries—for example, how to avoid "pushing" a prophetic word on others and to hold it loosely instead, trusting God with the results.

3. **Acknowledge them.** Intercessors should neither be ignored nor suppressed. Rather, pastors should acknowledge them—and that involves respecting and listening to them. Excited intercessors who feel strongly that they have heard from God can appear controlling, and this can be intimidating at times. But that's no reason for a wise pastor to discount, dismiss or avoid them.

4. **Communicate with them.** It's important for pastors to have intercessors who pray specifically for them—personal intercessors who "hold up our hands" in prayer as Aaron and Hur did for Moses (see Ex. 17:10-13). There are times when a prayer warrior may hold the key to something

critical we are about to face, so we need to make sure lines of communication are open.

The intercessors who pray for Alice and me receive a "prayer letter" from us each month. In this letter we share our blessings, triumphs, burdens and failures. Alice and I consider our personal intercessors integral to our health and to the success of our ministries.

We also give them access to us. My intercessors usually find it easy to get my attention—and I'm a better minister as a result. While preparing this article for example, I found myself in a perplexing situation. I needed a favor from a well-known church leader; however, a mutual friend advised me not to contact the leader until he had spoken with him first to introduce me and explain my need.

As soon as I hung up the phone, another friend called. "No need to wait for an introduction," he said, "I know the man well. He'll be quite open to your request."

Torn over how to proceed, I turned on my computer to go through my e-mail messages. I noticed that one message in particular was from Robin White, one of our personal intercessors. It was very simple, "Pastor Eddie," she wrote, "while praying for you and Alice this morning I felt I heard the Lord say, 'If in doubt, don't.' Love, Robin."

Respecting my intercessor, I did not call that leader but waited for the introduction to be made. When I told the story to my friend later, he said: "I am so glad you waited! The leader you wanted to contact had a bad experience recently that made him entirely closed to your request until I had the opportunity to talk with him about you."

Once again God used one of my intercessors to keep me on target!

5. **Affirm and encourage them.** Intercessors need to know they are a valued part of the church's ministry. They need to be told when they are right. And while they have no desire for undue attention that would provoke pride in them and jealousy in others, occasional honor—like that given to faithful Sunday school teachers, home group pastors, deacons or musicians—can sometimes be in order. Many intercessors feel misunderstood and can be insecure. Expressing gratitude to them and for them is a great encouragement.

6. **Love them.** Intercessors need affection. They need to know that we love them unconditionally, even when we disagree with their "word." We prove this by showing brotherly love and kindness to them and their families. (Alice and I try to communicate our love through occasional notes, postcards and so on).

Of course, pastors must use caution in this area. No pastor should ever become emotionally, personally or privately involved with someone of the opposite sex—regardless of that person's call, gifts or position in the church.

7. **Empower them.** Our intercessors are our ministry partners. God promised that those who receive a prophet will receive a prophet's reward (Matt. 10:41). Alice and I fully expect that any reward we receive will be accounted to those who have upheld us in prayer. Only God knows how much of our success is the result of their labor in the prayer closet for us!

8. **Cover them.** Prayer warriors need us to provide accountability and a safe place for them to pursue their callings and grow in their gifts. Because intercession is "heavenly" in focus, pastors must help ensure it is balanced with more "earthly" ministries. I sometimes have to remind the intercessors of my church that Jesus engaged in various activities between His prayer times: He healed the sick, cast out demons, raised the dead and fed the hungry, among other things! I also have to help them guard against any tendency to use their prayer closets as an escape from the normal realities of life.

In The on-going prayer of the Church should be one of repentance and desire for a fresh awakening to life in Christ. The Lord said that in the latter days He would pour out His Spirit on all flesh. Whether this fulfillment of prophecy is around the corner or some time away, let us pray that the Lord will move on our land in this way. providing a covering, however, it is critical that pastors discern between impurity and immaturity. Every prayer warrior is at a different level of maturity in Christ. And because intercessors tend to focus on the spiritual battle and the victory at hand, they often fail to consider the pitfalls or dangers.

Pastors, on the other hand, focus on safety; their goal is not only to win the battle but also to protect the flock. A mature intercessor will understand his pastor's heart and work *with* not *around* him. Likewise, a secure pastor will neither overvalue nor undervalue an intercessor, but rather will evaluate each one soberly, according to the measure of faith God has given him (see Rom. 12:3).

Sometimes an immature intercessor musters the courage to share with his pastor what he thinks God may be saying to him, only to be chastised, scolded or punished. How discouraging! Immature believers should never be treated as if they are impure; they should be lovingly encouraged.

We must make it clear that we will never dishonor or humiliate our intercessors. An open rebuke is uncalled for unless there has been a repeated pattern of rebellion or unteachability. Even then, all discipline should be administered in the love of Christ.

We can provide a safe place for intercessors to learn, and we can equip them to be our partners in ministry. It's worth our time, attention and effort. As more and more of us learn to partner with the intercessors in our churches, we will soon see the results: powerful and effective ministries in the name of Jesus that neither the church nor the world can ignore.

—Eddie Smith is cofounder, along with his wife, Alice, and president of the U.S. Prayer Center in Houston, Texas. Before starting the U.S. Prayer Center in 1990, Eddie and his wife Alice served 16 years in itinerant evangelism, and 14 years in the local church.

Reprinted with permission from Ministry Today, September/October 1997. Copyright Strang Communications Co., USA. All rights reserved

LESSON 12

PREPARING FOR THE COMING REVIVAL

MAIN PRINCIPLE

The on-going prayer of the Church should be one of repentance and desire for a fresh awakening to life in Christ. The Lord said that in the latter days He would pour out His Spirit on all flesh. Whether this fulfillment of prophecy is around the corner or some time away, let us pray that the Lord will move on our land in this way.

HOW TO FOLLOW GOD'S VOICE - IN INTERCESSION

PRAYER—OUR HIGH PRIVILEGE

by F.J. Huegel

It has often been said that prayer is the greatest force in the universe. That is no exaggeration. Prayer releases the immeasurable wealth and power of almighty God: "Call unto me, and I will answer thee and show thee great and mighty things, which thou knowest not."[1]

There we have it: "I will show you great and mighty things."[2] It is the voice of God. It is the omnipotent Sovereign, Creator and Sustainer of a hundred million universes, who here gives us his word. He with whom nothing is impossible, who spoke and worlds without number came into being, pledges his most holy and immutable word that if we will but seek his face in prayer, he will work and bring to pass great and mighty things such as have never been entertained in our minds.

We should not minimize the importance of other forms of service in the establishment of the Kingdom of God, but we must admit that prayer is the foremost weapon: "The weapons of our warfare are not carnal, but mighty through God."[3] Prayer must undergird all forms of Christian service if they are to be truly fruitful.

We can do good things and bless others without prayer; but God's ends, wherein eternal good is found, cannot be so achieved. We see an example in the life of our Lord Jesus. He initiated nothing without waiting prayerfully on the Father.

He laid down an unvarying principle, saying, "The Son can do nothing of himself, but what he seeth the Father do."[4] Prayer with the Son of man was as the very breath of life. As he stood beside Lazarus' tomb, Jesus said, "Father, I thank thee that thou hast heard me. And I know that thou hearest me always."[5] His closing word on the cross was a prayer.[6] And we are told that "he ever lives to make intercession for us."[7]

Prayer is not only our highest privilege and our most cherished joy (for thereby we hold communion with him who is the Fountain of Life), but it is also our most effective weapon whereby we may achieve.

All else leaves us floundering in the muck and the chaos of self-effort, which has never been anything but a blind alley. All else leaves us as a frail bark on life's stormy seas without a helm, without a compass, without a pilot.

If we build without direction from the Most High, who orders all according to an eternal plan (here is the highest definition of prayer, whereby we listen to God and receive strength to obey), our labors, however brilliant, must finally come to naught.

It is the one who does the will of God who abides forever.[8] Prayer in its truest form, its deepest and most worthy expression, brings our little effort into a harmonious blend with the great pattern and purposes of the Father of Lights and thereby gives to our otherwise puny achievements everlasting glory and meaning.

Prayer is work of such a sublime order that it lies beyond the imagination. For when the Christian prays, his capacity to achieve and his power to do good are multiplied a thousand fold, yea, a hundred thousand fold.

Witness Moses standing in the breach and praying for forgiveness for the children of Israel when, because of the worship of the golden calf, God's wrath was kindled and he purposed to destroy Israel.[9]

Witness the ministry of prayer of the great intercessors of the Bible. Witness the achievements of the George Mullers and the David Brainerds and the Amy Carmichaels of the Church.

Furthermore, when we pray, we are no longer hemmed in within the circle of a merely human sphere of activity. Our tiny scope, as we seek to do good and to bless people in need of the redemptive liberation of the Gospel of Christ, becomes as vast as the life of the nations.

> "THROUGH PRAYER WE CAN TOUCH THE ENDS OF THE EARTH."

When we preach, we may bless a congregation of believers; but when we pray, our capacity to bless is without limit. We may pray, as we are admonished to do, for all the saints,[10] and consequently bless a hundred million believers—yea, all the members of the Body of Christ. It is no longer we, but the One who sustains the universe, whose power to bless knows no bounds.

Through prayer we can touch the ends of the earth. Prayer makes it possible for us to open a beneficent and an immeasurably bountiful hand to bless people in distant lands. What a staggering fact!

Jesus our Lord, in his high priestly prayer, prayed for all those who should believe on him.[11] His prayer embraced the ages. So too our prayers may bless peoples yet unborn. On our knees we may thrust forth missionaries to the farthermost reaches of a sin-stricken humanity's heathenism; we may visit every prison and be a bearer of light to people who weep secretly. In the throes of endless night; we may visit every brothel in all the cities of the world to snatch souls from the flames of everlasting shame and bring them to the One who forgave the woman who kissed his sacred feet and washed them with her tears.

Lest you think that I am indulging in mad hyperbole, read what the Savior said in Luke 10:2 and in John 15:7. With God neither time nor space are barriers. He can work immediately in the hearts of people everywhere. Did not the Savior say, speaking of the coming of the Holy Spirit, that the Spirit would convict the world of sin?[12] And are we not given to understand that it is not the Father's will for any to perish?[13] And is it not written that Christ the Lord is the propitiation for the sins of the entire world?[14]

It is when we bow the knee and call on God that in a sense we become mighty: "Call unto me, and I will answer thee, and show thee great and mighty things, which thou knowest not."[1]

"You pray," says Almighty God, "and I will work. If you ask anything in My name, I will do it."[15] ..."Call upon me in the day of trouble: I will deliver thee, and thou shalt glorify me."[16]

"Come," he says in effect, "bow the knee and call on Me. As you pray, I will work. I pledge My omnipotence. You may not see at once any change, though there are times when before my people call, I answer. If you will but believe and wait on Me, all things will be possible; the very course of history may be changed, for with Me nothing is impossible."[17]

(1) Jeremiah 33:3, KJV. (2) Cf. Jeremiah 33:3. (3) 2 Corinthians 10:4, KJV. (4) John 5:19, KJV. (5) John 11:41-42, KJV. (6) Luke 23:46. (7) Cf. Hebrews 7:25. (8) 1 John 2:17. (9) Exodus 32:30-34. (10) Ephesians 6:18. (11) John 17:20. (12) John 16:8. (13) 2 Peter 3:9. (14) 1 John 2:2. (15) Cf. John 14:13-14. (16) Psalm 50:15, KJV. (17) Cf. Isaiah 65:24; cf. Matthew 19:26; cf. Luke 1:37

—Frederick J. Huegel was an author and missionary to Mexico. He wrote the classic *Bone of His Bone* and other books, including *Forever Triumphant, The Ministry of Intercession and Reigning with Christ*.

Taken from *Prayer's Deeper Secrets* by Fred Julius Huegel. Copyright © 1959 by Zondervan Publishing House. Used by permission of Zondervan.

HOW TO FOLLOW GOD'S VOICE - IN INTERCESSION

LOVING ENOUGH TO INTERCEDE

by Barbie Eslin

Back in 1992 when our pastor, Jamie Buckingham, was at the peak of his fight against cancer, our congregation rallied together in one accord, beseeching God for a miracle.

We frequently huddled together in special prayer services, pleading with God for Jamie's life. Around-the-clock prayer teams were posted. We received numerous calls to intercede during each phase of his treatment.

We fasted. We prayed. A bunch of us even marched around Jamie's house seven times.

After Jamie's death, I had to relearn *why* God wants us to pray. After all, we'd spent so much time "doing" it; why didn't it work? Hadn't we followed the right formulas, pulled all the right strings?

The interesting thing about praying in a crisis—indeed, the disturbing thing—is that we often focus our prayers based on our own perception of who or what is important. Frankly, we're not so concerned about who or what is important to God, but to *us*.

I still remember the murmurs that echoed throughout the church while Jamie lay ill: "Gee, I'm nobody. If I got cancer, who'd go to all this trouble for me?"

Good question.

Looking for an intercessor. Until our little kingdom blew up, "intercession" was little more to me than another spiritual buzz word for "prayer." I battled with inner frustration: "If God knows everything anyway, why should I even bother to pray?"

Suffice it to say that the subject of prayer became *the* focus of my conversations with God. Just what did God want from us—from me?

Then the fiery brand of God's Spirit burned a permanent mark on me, forever changing my heart and perspective on the church's call to "pray without ceasing" (1 Thess. 5:17).

During personal devotions, my eyes rested on a familiar passage in Isaiah 59: "The Lord looked and was displeased that there was no justice. He was appalled that there was no one to intervene (intercede); so His own arm worked salvation for Him, and His own righteousness sustained Him" (v. 15-16, NIV).

God pierced my heart as I realized what He must have felt when He searched and could not find *even one* willing to stand in the gap.

In an instant, the veil of complacency was torn in two as I saw the heart of God behind His call to believers to pray for one another. How sad He must be over the church's lack of *agape* love.

To pray—to be willing to intervene in diligent, compassionate and persistent prayer—we must love one another. Because if we don't love, we won't pray.

> WE IN THE CHURCH MUST LEARN TO LOVE ONE ANOTHER SO MUCH THAT WE AUTOMATICALLY CHOOSE TO STOP EATING, GET IN OUR PRAYER CLOSET AND SEEK GOD'S FACE AT HIS PROMPTING.

On Shaky ground. It's not fun to be an intercessor. It takes sacrifice, commitment, humility. You sacrifice meals. You commit to continue praying alone in your private "closet" about things you often have no full knowledge of—in obedience to that inner prompting.

And sometimes, when God leads, you step onto that shaky ground of speaking encouragement to the person you've been praying for, knowing that you risk being misunderstood.

Maybe that's why intercessors should never enter into prayer lightly. Like an evangelist friend said recently. "I'm scared to death most of the time." I, too, am scared of my own humanness and overwhelmed with awe because God cared enough to send His own intercessor, Jesus Christ, to an unworthy people—a people with no heart for prayer.

That amazing love, that sacrifice! It's the purpose of intercession that comes from glimpsing God's love.

We in the church must learn to love one another so much that we automatically choose to stop eating, get in our prayer closet and seek God's face at His prompting. We must learn to do so not because of who those persons are, or what they've accomplished in the kingdom, but because God loves them, and we know He desires to touch their lives.

Will it forever take a crisis to get the church to pray?

If we ever choose to be obedient to the prompting of the Holy Spirit to such a degree, maybe then we as leaders can preach, teach and model what praying "without ceasing" really means.

Why should I intercede? The very thought of God searching high and low for me to pray and not finding me is more than I can bear.

—Barbie Eslin is a writer and blogger. She is currently a freelance copywriter in the Health & Wellness and Christian markets. She was formally the associate editor of Ministry Today/Charisma Media.

Reprinted with permission from Ministry Today, January/February 1994. Copyright Strang Communications Co., USA. All rights reserved.

ZOE COURSE DESCRIPTIONS

"My sheep hear My voice, and I know them, and they follow Me." John 10:27 (KJV)

HEARING COURSES

Hearing God's Voice

In this course, everyone is encouraged to participate by applying the principles they read in scripture in order to learn to recognize when the Holy Spirit is speaking. The inner knowing, inner voice, and the authoritative voice of the Holy Spirit are discussed, as well as other manifestations of the Holy Spirit. The Lord is personal and unique, and desires to communicate with each one of His sheep in a personal and unique manner! (This course is a prerequisite for all the following courses except for How to Hear God's Voice—In Marriage.)

How To Hear God's Voice—In Christ

In the Hearing God's Voice course we learned how to hear God as individuals, whereas in the In Christ course, we learn how the body of Christ operates together under His direction and to His glory. We look at Romans 12 and examine the motive gifts that determine our individual bents. This study enables us to understand, appreciate and love each other. We also look at the Trinity and how they operate together. We learn about the precious person of the Holy Spirit and how He teaches, guides and comforts us. We also learn about the gifts of the Holy Spirit in 1 Corinthians 12 and 14 brought about as the Holy Spirit moves through us. Participants have remarked that this course has enabled them to see people the way God sees them and how they fit in the body of Christ.

How To Hear God's Voice—In Marriage

This course is based on the love relationship God had with mankind in the very beginning. We examine our attitudes toward each other and how they reflect the greatest love of all, the love of Christ. Do we love and honor each other with the unconditional love that our Lord Jesus had for us while dying on the cross? As in previous classes, we examine scripture, seek the Lord, and ask Him, "How can I better serve and love my spouse?" We discover how we complete each other, not compete with each other.

How To Hear God's Voice—In the Family

In today's society we see the growing deterioration of the family. Parents are confused about what the Bible teaches on family issues. During this course we examine scriptures and what it means to: "Train up a child [early childhood] in the way he should go [and in keeping with his individual bent], and when he is old [teen years can be the best] he will not depart from it." (AMP with additions)

KNOWING COURSES

How To Know God's Voice—In Intimate Friendship

Intimate Friendship with God! Can we experience such a relationship with the Creator of the universe? Here we examine what the Bible teaches us about the fear of the Lord, and how we can, indeed, have a deeper, more intimate relationship with Him. This is a very personal, yet freeing course on growing intimacy with God.

How To Know God's Voice—In Worship

The focus of this course is on ministering to the Lord. During our time together the Lord draws us corporately into His presence as we worship Him. We study what worship is, why we worship, and how we worship.

How To Know God's Voice—In His Presence

The Lord is calling each one of His sheep to come into His presence and to know Him in a deeper way. This course is not for the new believer nor the faint in heart. Those who are serious about knowing the Father in a more intimate way will find this class challenging but rewarding. Examining Jesus' last days on earth will direct us into the presence of the Lord. This class is for those who have completed other ZOE classes.

How To Know God's Voice—In the Coming of the Lord

Many are proclaiming dates and times when the Lord Jesus will return for His bride. This class is designed to focus on our preparation for His coming, not when He is coming, and to better understand the Lord's statement of Revelation 22:20: "Yes, I am coming." It is the goal of this course to prepare ourselves as the bride of Christ, with hearts that will respond with "Amen. Come, Lord Jesus."

FOLLOWING COURSES

How To Follow God's Voice—In Power

Evangelism is often thought of as a bad word! In this course we come to realize that God has a special plan for evangelism for us if we are only sensitive and obedient to His voice. Preparing your testimony, leading someone in salvation, and discipling others are a few of the topics discussed in this course. This is a real life-changer as we minister in "power evangelism!"

How To Follow God's Voice—In Healing

During this course we examine the scriptures in which Jesus healed the sick. The Holy Spirit highlights these passages as we study, and our faith increases! We realize that Jesus is the Healer, and we are simply His vessels as we listen to and follow His voice.

How To Follow God's Voice—In Intercession

Jesus is in constant intercession (Hebrews 7:25). As we come before Him in worship, intercession is a natural outflow of our relationship with Him. By yielding to the Holy Spirit, our ministry to others through intercession will increase.

How To Follow God's Voice—In Spiritual Warfare

As we come to know and recognize who our Lord is, He reveals to us who He is not! The tactics of Satan and our spiritual weapons are defined in this class. The Lord leads us in spiritual warfare as He enlists and mobilizes His army!

ONE-ON-ONE DISCIPLESHIP

Discipleship by the Word and the Holy Spirit

This 12-week course was developed by a disciple-maker after many years of successful one-on-one discipleship. Through this method the Holy Spirit is allowed to minister to the disciple through the Word and the encouragement of the disciple-maker. No other techniques or methods are used.

The entire course has been designed to enable individuals to feel confident in making disciples as directed by our Lord: *"Therefore go and make disciples of all nations…." Matthew 28:19.*

Not only do participants learn what discipleship means according to the Word of God, but they are encouraged to participate in a one-on-one discipleship program as part of the course. This training allows individuals to take great strides in their personal relationship with God and in ministry. It changes lives in a very simple, yet powerful way.

EVANGELISTIC OUTREACH — MINISTRY IN HOMES

Captivated by Their Character

This series of courses called Captivated by Their Character is designed to reach the unbeliever, new believer, and those needing a refresher course on the Trinity.

They are offered in a non-threatening, home atmosphere where every effort is made to make the participant feel comfortable with the material. For example, everyone uses the same Bible, referring to page numbers rather than books, no reading is required outside of the course, and they are given the freedom to express their inadequacies as a believer or non-believer.

The three 6-week courses in the Captivated by Their Character series are titled Who Is Jesus?, Who Is God the Father? and Who Is the Holy Spirit?

Additional information is available on the website at www.zoeministires.org/zoe-courses

MAGAZINE LIST

For your convenience we have included the following list of magazines from which this course's articles have been drawn. If you wish to receive these magazines on a regular basis, the subscription information below will help.

A Great Love, Inc.
P.O. Box 1248
Toccoa, GA 30577

(800) (706) 886-5161
www.24-7prayusa.org

Charisma and Christian Life
Subscription Service Department
P.O. Box 420234
Palm Coast, FL 32142-0234

(800) 829-3346
www.charismamag.com

Christ For the Nations
P.O. Box 769000
Dallas, TX 75376-9000

(800) 933-CFNI
www.cfni.org

Decision Magazine
Billy Graham Evangelistic Association
P.O. Box 668886
600 Rinehart Road
Lake Mary, FL 32746

(877) 247-2426
www.ministrytodaymag.com

Equipping the Saints
Vineyard USA
P.O. Box 2089
Stafford, TX 77497

(281) 313-8463
www.vineyardusa.org

Ministry Today
Magazine Customer Service
600 Rinehart Road
Lake Mary, FL 32746

(407) 333-0600
www.ministrytodaymag.com

Times Square Church Pulpit Series
c/o World Challenge
P.O. Box 260
Lindale, TX 75771

(903) 963-8626
www.worldchallenge.org

Made in the USA
Middletown, DE
23 July 2023